Yankees in the Cornfield

Emmett Snead

Copyright © 2017 Emmett Snead

All rights reserved.

ISBN-13: 978-0-9995856-0-3

DEDICATION

This book is dedicated to my mother, Jane F. Snead, the real unsung hero of Braehead Farm.

PRAISE FOR YANKEES IN THE CORNFIELD

"If you've ever yearned to return to a time before smartphones, social media and e-mail, this is the book for you. Slip into a simpler time and enjoy this fictional tale from real-life 1960s Fredericksburg."
-Glenn Markwith, Colonial Beach, Va.

"Emmett's personality and character flow through the pages as though he is actually speaking to you. It was fascinating to read this fictional tale inspired by his early years. Everett's character developed through a strict upbringing and hard work. The experience encouraged him to be very industrious and enterprising. When he realizes that not everyone has been raised this way, the comparisons can be quite hilarious."
-Judy Jones, Queensland, Australia

"My grandparents owned a dairy farm in Fauquier County, which I visited on Sunday afternoons. ... I learned so much more about the hard work of a farmer and really appreciate them even more since this reading! ... Growing up in the Fredericksburg area, I enjoyed the walks down Memory Lane in the stories of cruising between Hardees and the Hot Shoppes and other landmarks of our youth that are now gone."
Gaynelle Chewning Scott, Fredericksburg, Va.

"*Yankees in the Cornfield* captures the feel of East Coast farm life in post-World War II America. It's as wholesome and organic as the experience itself—until the turn of a page turns the story."
-Phil Harding, Fredericksburg, Va.

"This book would be enjoyed by anyone who grew up in Fredericksburg, recalling how life was back in the day, when our community was smaller and life was simpler."
-Robert B.P. Thompson, Fredericksburg, Va.

"A lot of things in this book remind me of growing up in Fredericksburg."
- Larry Silver, Boca Raton, Fla.

"The book paints a vivid portrait of a farm boy's youth growing up in rural Virginia. As the plot develops, the reader is taken on a wild ride of adventures just one step over or under the line! Everett and his best friend are ace shots, have endless energy and know how to out-best the seasoned fishermen on the Rappahannock River, just to name a few of their talents. This is a suspenseful, refreshing and fun read about rural boys in the 1960s. The Baby Boomer generation will love it and long for their youth without technology."
- Beryl and Dick Carland, Minneapolis, Minn.

"If you want to feel and understand life in a small Southern city in the mid-1900s, read *Yankees in the Cornfield*. Times do change, but we should all be aware of our past and not forget where we came from."
-Chip Schwab, Marietta, Ohio

"The way basketball is combined with farming makes for interesting storytelling."
-"Coach" Drake, Louisburg, N.C.

"Having grown up on a farm in the 1960s, the book makes me jealous of the way Everett was able to blend work with play."
-Bob Massey, Spotsylvania County, Va.

CONTENTS

	Foreword	1
1	The Attack	3
2	The Aftermath	6
3	Minnesota	10
4	Dragonflies, Witch Doctors and Scorpions	14
5	Squirrel Hunting	17
6	Bruno	19
7	Poachers	22
8	Basketball, a.k.a. "The Long Ball"	24
9	Winter	27
10	Hard Work's Not Easy	29
11	Blizzards and Dairy Cows	31
12	My Favorite Ex-Con	36
13	Springtime in the Rappahannock River Valley	42
14	Barefoot Green	46
15	Yankees in the Cornfield	51
16	Whistle Pigs	54
17	Leslie Chased	56
18	Paris Inn	59

19	Opening Silage Fields	62
20	Fall	66
21	Dove Hunting	68
22	The Mystery Bag	72
23	Persimmon Trees	75
24	Metes and Bounds	78
25	Used Batteries	81
26	Drug-Oriented Hippie Music	86
27	Servicetown	91
28	Night Vision	94
29	The Intruder	96
30	Cloud Cover	100
31	Leslie's Day Off	102
32	Rye Behind Corn	104

This book is a work of historical fiction with feeling, set in a real place and time.

Before there were strip malls and the Internet.
Before the federal government promoted farming "fencerow to fencerow" to export grain to Russia.
Before having children was considered a luxury because they were <u>needed</u> to be part of the workforce.
What was life like growing up on a family farm and coming of age near a small dormant town in Virginia?
How did farmers farm and what were their methods?
Add in sexual assault, revenge and murder, then the story becomes a myth sliced from the historical pages of the 1960s.
For Baby Boomers who grew up in the '60s, that time in history has become legendary!

FOREWORD

Yankees in the Cornfield is a book that will take you inside of the mind and the world of a young Southern farm boy growing up in the Virginia of the 1960s. It harks back to a time that, on its surface, seems simpler, with small-town children growing up doing chores, hunting and fishing, and having adventures. Under the surface, however, lies the undercurrent of racial tension, of a world standing on the cusp of the unknown and unseen future of a country that would soon be divided not by another civil war, but by a growing civil rights movement and the specter of the Vietnam War.

Young Everett Smith is awakened from sleep by a terrifying event, which, as a small child, he cannot completely understand. His life goes on as he grows up on a farm in small-town Fredericksburg, Va. Throughout his joyful, idyllic, often funny childhood, there lies residue of the unsolved mystery.

This book is not politically correct. Some may be offended by what they perceive as the portrayal of African-Americans as dumb or immoral, and others will likely be equally offended by the joy Everett and Frankie get from hunting and killing animals they define as "varmints." Emmett Snead has in this story placed Everett in the unvarnished and sometimes prejudiced and unattractive world in which he himself lived. This honesty has value even while it can make us wince as well as smile.

Emmett Snead both is and is not Everett Smith. This is a work of fiction and should be enjoyed as such. At the same time, Emmett draws on his childhood, and some of the stories in the book describe actual experiences and family legends of Emmett's own life.

Themes in this book revolve not only around racial tension in a society still with de facto segregation, but also around the definition of justice, as Everett struggles to define for himself what is really morally right or wrong. Another key theme focuses on the bonds of family across the generations. Everett's story is rich with the wealth of his relationships with his parents and grandparents. In fact, he wrote this book in no small part to share this sense of history with his own children and their descendants.

Enjoy this book for what it evokes: a sense of a time and place, evocative memories of food and popular music, the feeling of being a young boy in a world full of wonder and possibility. It is also a good story and a lot of fun. If you have been to Fredericksburg, Va., or are ever fortunate enough to visit, you will see some of the landmarks of Everett's childhood, although some no longer stand. Be prepared to have Everett Smith join Huckleberry Finn and Holden Caulfield in your heart as boys growing into men into a world that is both simple and complex.

So, welcome to the world of Everett Smith's youth. Sit back, have a Dr Pepper, and enjoy.

Dr. Rebecca Bigoney

1 THE ATTACK

Spring 1958

My eyes cracked open. I dared not move. I pretended to be asleep.

I had awakened from bottomless sleep in a lightning flash. Every hair on my body was raised in a frightful instant. The stench in my bedroom reeked of a combination of odors reminiscent of corn silage and liquor mixed with vomit, with a strong overriding aroma of gasoline. My instincts told me to hide anywhere—even under the sheets. I was completely exposed lying on top of my small bed.

The hall that divided my room from my parents' room was dimly lit with a low-wattage bulb. Our doorways were directly across from each other.

Against this faint light, I could make out a dark figure. It seemed rat-like in its movements, quick and jerking followed by halting stares in my direction. It seemed to be focused on my bureau as it slipped into my room.

I knew my dad was milking cows down at the barn. He always came into my room at 4 a.m., just before going to the barn. He would be sure to check to see if I was on my side, my feet pointing at a right angle to my body while I slept. The podiatrist had said that doing this while I was young might help my feet grow straight. I was born with them twisted and turned inward. He said I would never play sports. I was determined otherwise.

I knew I was all alone and in great danger.

There appeared to be some type of dangerous, stinking wild animal in my room, perhaps a new kind of varmint that needed to be killed. If my dad were here, he would have already shot it with his shotgun.

I had my own flock of chickens that I had raised from baby chicks. We were eating breakfast one morning when my chickens started squawking furiously. Without a word, my dad jumped up from the breakfast table, grabbed his shotgun from the bedroom and ran into the backyard. A stray dog was running away with a chicken in its mouth.

My dad fired once. The chicken fully recovered. The dog did not. My dad measured the kill distance at 75 yards.

I begged my father for a gun. I told him my best friend had a .22 rifle and his father let him hunt squirrels. He was also 7 years old, just like me. I was ready to kill varmints, but dad told me I was too young, and would have to wait till I was 13.

My dad was not here now.

The figure, watching me intently, snatched my piggy bank from the bureau and put it in his pocket.

He quickly scurried across the hall into my parents' bedroom.

I saw daylight breaking through the window of my parents' bedroom.

The varmint's outline next to my mother's dresser was clearly visible. It stuffed several dollars from inside the dresser into its pocket. I wanted to warn my mother, but did not know how to do so without drawing the attention of whatever it was that was in her bedroom.

A slight movement from my parents' bed caught its eye.

I was beginning to wonder whether my mother and I would see the sunrise again.

He was on her bed in one bound. One knee was in the middle of her back. His gasoline-smeared hand was over her mouth.

"Don't says a word, if ya wants to live!"

It was a man, not an animal after all!

She bit his middle finger all the way to the bone. With a loud, piercing scream, he recoiled backward, momentarily letting go.

Rolling over and lifting up both of her legs simultaneously as he was recoiling, she kicked with all her strength and weight. The impact caused the man to flip over backwards off the bed and onto the floor with a loud thud.

My mother cut loose with a loud screeching scream unlike any I had ever heard.

The man bounced from the floor in one movement and ran headlong down the hall toward the front door, a desperate look of panic and surprise on his face.

He was a black man with a light complexion and short hair.

I had never seen him before; I would never forget his face.

My mother was running behind him, all the while shrieking that unforgettable ear-piercing scream.

He never stopped running for as far as she could see him.

She stopped in the middle of our front yard next to the farm's dinner

bell. It was rusted and made of cast iron with a large, heavy clapper.
   Ten hard, quick rings sounded from the bell.
   Then silence.

2 THE AFTERMATH

Spring 1958

The morning milking had been going well, even though none of the workers had shown up. It was as though they planned when they would go on their drunks. That way neither one would have to do the work of the other. My dad was on his last "side" of milk cows to bring into the barn to be milked. A "side" was 15 cows—one side of the 30-cow milk barn. This barn was less than a year old and held 4,000 bales of alfalfa hay to be fed to the cows while they were being milked.

A contractor had built this barn, and it represented a huge investment into the future of the farm. It was called the "new barn." The milk sold from this barn would be grade A milk. Grade A milk brought twice as much per hundred weight over grade B milk. The milk herd had been increased from 45 to 60 cows. The math looked good on paper. My father planned to increase the herd to 100 cows. He also planned to buy another farm to raise more hay to feed the cows.

My grandfather had built the "old barn" himself almost 20 years earlier. It held only 15 milk cows and 2,000 bales of hay. The old barn was a solidly built and very functional barn, but it was obsolete and only grade B milk could legally be sold from the cows that were milked in it. In order to be approved by the government to sell grade A milk, the barn had to be brought up to their building code. There could not be any exposed loft floor rafters. The milk could no longer be water cooled in 10-gallon cans. It had to be stored in a large refrigerated vat with a paddle that kept it stirred. You could no longer haul milk to the creamery in 10-gallon cans. A driver with a refrigerated trailer truck had to be hired to haul the milk to the creamery.

After all, this was 1958.

Overall production of everything on the farm had exploded. My grandfather was 67 and had retired from his full-time job at the local Sylvania plant producing cellophane. That job, along with my grandmother's large fertile hen egg operation provided the cash flow for the dairy business. My grandfather at 67 could still do the work of any younger man. My dad at 37 was still seeking farming advice daily from my grandfather and grandmother.

My grandmother had graduated from what is now the University of Mary Washington in 1915 and had taught school until she got married. She ran the business end of the farm with my dad. My grandfather ran the farming end of the operation with my dad. Every one of his ancestors had been a farmer somewhere in Virginia since 1635. He knew farming on all levels. My mother had also graduated from UMW. She ran the household, picked the fruits and vegetables from our acre garden and froze or canned the excess. She also helped both my grandmothers in their day-to-day needs, which included being the designated gopher to run errands for the farm. My mom's dad was the manager of a fertilizer and grain purchasing facility company that adjoined our farm. He had graduated from Virginia Polytechnic Institute (now Virginia Tech) with an agriculture degree. I always looked forward to Sunday dinner at my mom's parent's house after church. It was an opportunity to meet and play with kids in town.

They were a good team. The farm was poised to really take off.

My father usually zoned out and was in deep thought while he milked cows, unless he was talking farming strategies with his dad.

Earlier my dad had told my grandfather that he was deeply concerned that someone had been stealing gas from the large gas tank used to keep the tractors running.

This concerned my grandfather. Once someone has the gall to come onto your farm and do petty theft, they are usually looking around to see what else they can steal. Theft was a serious problem on a farm he previously owned. A father and son stole his entire wheat crop from his barn that he had in 100-pound bags. They did it one Sunday morning while he was in church. It had rained the previous night, so when he came back from church he saw an unfamiliar set of tracks leading to his granary. At that time, all the roads in Spotsylvania County were dirt roads. He followed the tracks for several miles to another farm. He called the sherriff and got his wheat crop back. The thieves went to jail. Once they got out of jail, they came to church the next week and apologized to my grandfather.

My dad told my grandfather that he had been watching the gas tank from several points around the farm, but he had seen no one. The gasoline tank was situated nearby, between the milk barn and the barn lot.

My grandfather told my dad that the thief would be stealing the gas during the early morning milking while it was dark outside. That way the thief could watch their every move inside the lighted barn while stealing the gas in the dark outside. If anyone came in his direction, he would just lie down in the grass until they walked by.

My grandfather had farm dogs and suggested that my dad should get a dog or two. Right now, my dad was washing the cow bags, putting on the machines, milking the cows, and carrying the milk to the milk room. During this time, he was in deep thought on how to catch a thief he could not see. To make matters worse, the noise made by the milking machines made it hard to hear anything outside the milk barn.

My grandfather was in the barn lot bringing in the last side of cows to be milked that morning. He observed daylight was breaking and the sun would be up soon.

Suddenly, to his shock, he heard my mother screaming madly and the dinner bell ringing wildly.

He ran to the barn to where my father was, saying, "Something is bad wrong with Donna!" Not saying a word, my dad ran to the house, which was less than 100 yards away.

Arriving in the yard, he saw my mother holding the broken pull chain for the bell in her hand. The adrenaline had given her the strength to break the chain. Pointing across the plowed field she said, "He went that way!"

"Who?" my dad asked.

"I don't know."

As my dad was running into the house to get his shotgun, he said, "Call the police!" He instantly returned and startled tracking the intruder across the field. My grandfather, standing nearby, went back to the barn and finished the milking by himself. My mother called the police. My father tracked the intruder to the far side of the farm to where the heifers' pasture began and lost his tracks.

After calling the police, my mother was gazing out of the picture window watching my dad track the intruder across the plowed field out front. Dawn had broken. Suddenly, she was able to see a pair of shoes that had been placed neatly at the edge of the yard. The intruder had taken them off so as not to be heard while tip-toeing through the house.

When the police arrived with a bloodhound, my mother told them about the shoes. They used the shoes for the bloodhound to get the scent. The hound tracked the scent into the black section of town but eventually lost the scent.

My mother had locked the front and back doors. My parents had never locked up unless they left the farm. After all, we lived in the country where it was supposedly safe.

My mother was constantly pacing back and forth between the two doors to see if they were still locked. She did this for hours until my dad came back. She asked me, "Do you think the intruder is coming back?" "No," I said, no longer feeling afraid. "Not while my dad is out there with a shotgun!" I was standing in the living room, looking out the picture window at the front field, which had just been plowed. On a clay knoll, about a third of the way across the field, I saw two gas cans just sitting there. I surmised that the intruder had set down the two stolen gas cans while resting. Looking back at our house, he decided he wanted more than just the gas.

Our picture window faced east. The sun was rising. I had a bittersweet feeling. My mother and I would live another day.

3 MINNESOTA

Summer 1965

I was introduced to the surrealistic world of comic books in Minneapolis, Minn. I stayed there for three weeks one summer with my cousins. They lived in an upscale subdivision in the suburbs. Every house on the block had kids in it my age. All the kids ran in a pack. The mothers would take turns taking care of the pack. Every day, they planned a different outing. They were experts at having a good time without spending much, if any, money. Minneapolis was nothing like I had expected. Actually, I did not know what to expect. It turned out to be complete and utter culture shock. Up to that point, the only time I had been away from home was a week at 4-H camp.

Every other day, all summer, one mother would load up a station wagon, including packing kids into the back, and go to a nearby lake. Minnesota was known as the state of ten thousand lakes. The lake had an extensive beach and a large platform in the middle that you could swim out to. The water was clean and clear. There were several diving boards on the platform and a deck to lay out on.

We would have races out to the deck and spend hours diving off the diving board. We could all swim like fish.

I had learned to swim at a neighborhood pool in town not far from our farm. My parents had joined even though it was several miles away. It was convenient because one of my grandmothers lived in the neighborhood. I went to the pool anytime I wanted to, after I had completed all assigned chores. I went most every evening. If no one took me, I rode my bike there through a short cut on a path through a thickly wooded area called Alum Spring.

That lake was also the first place that I *really* started noticing girls. Older teenage girls would be sunbathing on the beach. Some of them had a lot of cleavage. One of my friends who had a very low voice would sing out, "I Like it Like That" by the Dave Clark Five. That song title became code for bikini sightings. Another cool song we liked at that time was "Love Potion No. 9" by the Searchers.

I introduced the game of Red Rover at the Minnesota lake. Everyone instantly loved that game. So much so that we would play it on land almost every night in my aunt's backyard. My aunt had the largest backyard in the neighborhood. It was close to an acre. She had assigned me the job of mowing the grass. My cousin was thrilled because he thought it to be such "hard work" and he did not have to do it anymore while I was visiting.

I never knew that grass was supposed to be mowed more than once per week. I always woke up around 6 a.m. To me, that was sleeping in. All the other kids woke up around 9 or 10. They were sleeping their lives away. In Virginia, life was too exciting to do a lot of sleeping. Of course, the adults were up. My uncle went to work at 8 a.m. He was a CPA. My aunt was a teacher and had the summer off. They had moved to Minnesota from Virginia because good teachers were paid more there than in any other state.

I would mow the grass every two or three days, depending on how much it rained. My aunt would watch me from the back door with a smile on her face. The job would take less than an hour to complete. I would then ask her if she had any more "jobs" to do. She seldom did. There was just not much work to do there.

Living there was very different from life on a farm. She had some rules to go by. My dad just had finish lines.

They did have a TV and a large record player. There was also a pool table in the basement.

Her rules were: only one hour per day of TV. That was one hour more than I had in Virginia. Only one hour per day of rock 'n' roll music could be played in the house. Again, another hour more than in Virginia.

All assigned "work" had to be completed first. You could play pool or read comic books for as long as you liked. No eating was allowed between meals. There were no allowances.

I could tell my mother and my aunt were cut from the same cloth. They were both frugal and experts at postponing instant gratification.

My aunt had a shoebox marked "vacation" with a hole cut into the top. Any time the family could save money, it would go into the box. The value of every Sunday evening's meal would be put into the box and everyone would eat just a bowl of cereal. She also saved money for vacations by buying powdered milk and mixing it with water. She also bought regular milk. She would mix the two together 50/50 for everyone to drink or put on cereal.

This was shocking to me, having grown up on a dairy farm.

I was accustomed to drinking a quart of whole milk every meal.

I learned to drink water that summer. My aunt told me whole milk was bad for your health. I responded by telling her it had stunted my growth. I was already taller than anyone on my mother's side of the family. She laughed and said, "clever boy."

Every payday, my uncle would put a small percentage of money in the box. Quarterly, the money would be counted. The family members would start planning where they could afford to go for their two weeks' vacation every year. It was always far away. Sometimes they would come to Virginia.

Sometimes, I would ask my mother for a "luxury item" when I was a kid. She was an expert at finding ways to come up with the money over a period of time during the spring and summer seasons without cutting into my father's farm money. She would help me pick extra produce from the garden to sell to people she knew in town. Strawberries were the best money maker. Once we saved up enough money to buy a croquet set. Another time a bicycle. This system of working and saving gave me the idea to sell produce and eggs door to door from my bicycle in town by the age of ten.

Going to Minnesota seemed like a real vacation to me! My female cousin loved Herman's Hermits. My uncle would make fun of Herman's Hermits by going around the house singing, "I'm Henry the 'Ape,' I am." I liked the Dave Clark Five. We took turns using the stereo. My male cousin taught me to play pool.

Luckily, I had brought a good amount of money I had earned selling eggs with me. I would pretend to go bike riding and hang out at a nearby burger joint. I would then go to Baskin-Robbins. The place was unbelievable. It had 31 flavors. Carl's in Fredericksburg only had 3. Baskin-Robbins even gave away ice cream. You got a membership punch card. For every ten scoops you bought, you would get one free scoop. They had these special wide cones that held 3 jumbo scoops. Every three and a third cones, I got a free scoop. I became their best customer.

One day after I came back from a bike ride, my aunt said, "I know you've been out wasting money on food."

"How do you know that?" I asked.

Every time you come back from a bike ride, your stomach is hanging out over your belt. Besides, all the mothers here have their eye on you.

I wasn't offended. In fact, I felt rather secure knowing everyone was watching out for me.

"If you take as good care of your pocketbook as you do your stomach, you'll be a very successful man in life," mused my aunt.

That sounded like a plan to me. There was a boy who lived across the street, two doors down. We became good friends. He introduced me to comic books. He had a stack of comic books as high as my knee. He would let me borrow as many as I wanted. The Kinks song, "All Day and All of the Night" applied to me reading comic books.

The comic book collector was very curious and very intelligent. He loved asking me questions about where I was from and how I lived. He was intrigued by the fact that there was a Roman numeral after my name. He was fascinated by my Southern accent and would ask me to say certain words over and over. I would ask him to speak "Yankee" and say certain words also. We would both laugh at each other until we cried.

He wanted to know why I referred to him as a Yankee. I explained to him about The War of Northern Aggression. He said he had never heard of such a thing. He loved hearing stories about Jeb Stuart and Mosby's Raiders. I recommended some books for him to check out the next time we went to the library. He said he liked the Civil War (as he came to call The War of Northern Aggression) books better than comic books. I had already read the books, so I liked the comic books better. We were both happy.

After several weeks, he asked me one day who won the war.

If you asked a Southerner, they'd say the South. If you asked a Yankee, it turns out that they won. We both laughed hysterically.

His parents never said much to me. They would stare at me as if I was from outer space with puzzled looks on their faces.

My aunt had warned me not to personalize "The Whaar Stories," but it was okay to generalize.

There were so many other things to do in Minneapolis on the days that we did not go to the lake. This included a trained seal show, acres and acres of flower gardens, the Minnesota State Fair, the local library, tubing down the Apple River, visiting a greenhouse, fishing at their cabin on a lake in the north country and going to the movies. We always went to church on Sunday.

It seemed like some type of a dream world the way people lived in subdivisions. There was one big problem with it. There was no way for a kid to make money. I had the time of my life, but I was glad to get back to Virginia.

4 DRAGONFLIES, WITCH DOCTORS AND SCORPIONS

Summer 1966

I had been taught from a very early age the importance of beneficial insects to agriculture and natural processes. This knowledge was imprinted onto my mind almost daily. Both sides of my family were strong advocates of beneficial insects. My mother would demonstrate this belief by going to great lengths to release helpful insects that had become trapped in the house back into the outside world. Even insects that were unknown to her or neutral for agricultural purposes would be "let go." However, insects that were known to be harmful or detrimental to crops were always crushed.

My dad believed that somehow our family could tip the scales in such a way that nature would work in our favor instead of against us while farming. He would say, "*Help nature to help you.*"

It made sense to me and it certainly didn't cost any money to let the beneficial insects kill the harmful insects.

Tobacco worms, also known as caterpillars, were nasty. They looked and sounded fierce. They had horns coming out from the top of their head and were three to four inches long. They were a little over half an inch wide and exactly the same color as a tomato plant. They were almost impossible to see because they were so well-camouflaged. There were two ways to find them. First, I would look for their droppings underneath a tomato plant, which would be about half the size of an eraser on a No. 2 pencil. Second, I would shake the tomato plant. The caterpillars would immediately start making a loud clicking noise with their large mandibles that they used to devour tomatoes and tomato plants. I would pick up two clods of dirt and smack them together with the worm in the middle, being careful to do the deed at an angle where the green juices—which were plentiful—did not land on my face or clothing. I was about to crush a tobacco worm when I noticed two rows of what appeared to be small white eggs down the length of his back. I called my dad over and showed him the worm. He said to never kill a tobacco worm when I noticed eggs on its back because they are the eggs of parasitic wasps that would do the job for me. As time goes on, the eggs would grow bigger, drawing their sustenance from the caterpillar. By the time the baby parasitic wasps are ready to hatch out, the caterpillar has been sucked dry and is dead. At that point, there are several dozen wasps ready to lay eggs on several dozen more tobacco worms. It was interesting to see how many tobacco worms would become colonized.

There were many other beneficial insects. Some were harder to promote than others because of the general ignorance of our workers. My dad had decided that he would be their teacher. Our black workers thought that praying mantises were the "witch doctors" of the insect world and that the claws on their "hands" were poisonous. They would also refer to blue-tailed lizards as scorpions because they could "throw" their tail off and if it hit you, the tip of the tail would "sting" you. Dad would pick up a praying mantis while they were watching. He would hold it by its legs whereupon it would defend itself by "clawing" at his fingers. After a few minutes, he would let it go and show everyone that his fingers were not bleeding, nor was he poisoned. He would catch a lizard and hold it in his hand while it "threw" its tail. After letting the lizard go, he would cup his hand while the lizard's separated tail would thrash around crazily. He would explain this was a tactic the lizard had evolved to fool predators into going after its tail instead of its body. Lizards were excellent fly and insect catchers, as were praying mantises.

The workers thought all snakes were copperheads that needed to be killed on sight. My father tried in vain to explain that black snakes were non-poisonous and were our friends because of all the vermin that they killed. Finally, the only way he could stop them from killing black snakes was to fire them on the spot.

Also, everyone wanted to kill all bees because all bees would sting. Some bees were of little or no value, such as paper wasps and especially yellow jackets. The bees that my dad would educate workers on as beneficial were honeybees, hornets and various wild bees that were pollinators. Honeybees were not only valued for the honey they made but also for being pollinators. Besides spiders, hornets were one of the few natural enemies of houseflies. Hornets would fly slowly up and down the walls of the milk barn looking for houseflies or horse flies that had lit on the wall. Upon spotting its prey, the hornet would accelerate its flying speed and quickly "grab" the fly from behind with its six legs, pinning its prey's wings. The hornet would carry the caught insect back to its nest to feed its larvae.

During the summer, I had always noticed dragonflies. They seemed to be in every type of habitat that had an open field: swampy fields, hay fields and crop fields. They appeared to be flying around erratically, sort of willy-nilly with no purpose.

Enlightenment came one summer morning about an hour after sunrise. I had been looking for an errant milk cow while walking across a pasture in a westerly direction. I turned to look back across the pasture into the direction of the rising sun. There were many swarms of tiny insects rising out of the dewy pasture resembling miniature whirlwinds. Dozens of dragonflies were flying into the swarms snagging insects and then would abruptly turn and come back and snag some more insects. With its biplane-type wings, the dragonfly could match its prey zig for zag, causing it to look like it was flying willy-nilly, when actually it was feeding on tiny insects that I could not see. The early morning angle of the sun allowed me to see the little insects that were invisible in full daylight. The feeding frenzy of the dragonflies reminded me of Jacques Cousteau TV shows that I saw at my grandmother's house, where predator fish would feed on schools of sardines by swimming rapidly into the schools, snagging a fish and then making a hard turn to come back to the school of fish and repeating the process.

The good news was that no one wanted to harm dragonflies.

5 SQUIRREL HUNTING

Late Summer 1966

Ever since last year's hunting season had ended, I had wanted a new squirrel gun. On my 10th birthday, my dad had given me a single-shot .22 rifle. Because of the attack on my mother and the constant pleading for a gun, my dad moved up the date for me having my own gun from 13 to 10 years old. I was excited. Strings were attached, however. The gun had to be treated as though it was always loaded and only pointed toward the ground or up toward the sky. I had to keep it clean and buy my own ammo.

I had saved up my egg, vegetable and asparagus money for more than a year.

Now I was 14, and that seemed like a long time ago.

My friend Frankie had a semiautomatic .22. I had complained to my dad, and he had answers ready as usual. "Single-shot guns are safer," he claimed. "They make you learn to make every shot count. Since Frankie has everything now, he won't have anything to look forward to once he gets older. Buy your own gun, you'll appreciate it more."

I decided to take his advice and buy my own gun. My mother had lent me her double-barrel .410. It was a nice gun. It did not kick much, and always had two shots. At close range, it was deadly for squirrels. I had even shot one squirrel in mid-air while it was jumping from one tree to another. A squirrel out of shotgun range required the use of a rifle.

Sometimes I took the single-shot .22 rifle hunting. I became skilled at picking squirrels off at a distance if they were motionless. If a squirrel saw me, it would run full-speed to a hiding place. They almost always saw me before I saw them, and they had excellent hearing. I would hunt after milking. I only had a couple hours before dusk. During this time, I would kill two or three squirrels. Our forest was perfect habitat for squirrels. The trees in the forest were past the peak growth stage. Instead of the trees making better timber, they were in decline. This means that the trees were hollowing out and becoming habitats for squirrels and other animals. There was a mix of many different varieties of nut trees including oaks, hickories, and walnuts.

On most Saturdays, my dad went to the Fredericksburg Hardware store downtown. It was also located next to the farmers' market. He liked to stock up on whatever we did not have in the garden. He also liked to talk to the other farmers in the hardware store. My grandfather *never* stood around talking to other farmers. I found other farmers' conversations to be boring too.

"I got a half an inch of rain Wednesday night," said the first farmer.

"I got three quarter-inches of rain Wednesday night," said the second farmer.

"I got over one inch of rain Wednesday night," said the third farmer.

Sometimes I wondered if they got any rain at all. I used the opportunity to go on the other side of the store to the hunting section. I had had my eye on a specific gun for a while now. It was an unusual gun. It was called an over-under. It had two barrels, one over top of the other. The top barrel was a .22 magnum, which was significantly more powerful than a .22 rifle. The bottom barrel was a 20-gauge shotgun, with significantly more power than a .410 shotgun. It would be a perfect varmint and squirrel gun. I would have killing power at close range or long range. The gun was still there and for sale.

I proudly laid down $52.50 and announced to the clerk which gun I wanted. Without question, he retrieved the gun for me. I then purchased a generous amount of ammo. Walking back to where my dad was talking with the other farmers, I announced, "let's go home so I can target practice!" My dad, looking quite surprised, said, "I'll meet you in the truck in a few minutes."

That always meant at least a half hour.

6 BRUNO

Fall 1966

I did enough target practicing by hunting season to feel very comfortable with my new gun. I had already passed my driver's license test the day I turned 15. The year before, my dad brought home a new German Shepherd puppy named Bruno. I took him target practicing with me. I started off shooting ammunition called .22 shorts. The noise they made was not much more than a pop. I did this for a number of target-shooting sessions until he basically ignored the shooting noise. I then moved up to .22 longs. They were a little louder. Then to .22 long rifles which were the loudest and made a cracking noise. He was becoming very tolerant to gunshots.

Most recently, I had taken Bruno target shooting with my new gun, which was loudest of all. He had become tolerant of the noise of gunshots of my new over and under .22-magnum gun.

I now had a dog that, unlike most dogs, was not gun shy. It was a major accomplishment!

While target practicing, I would fantasize that the bullseye was the face that I had never forgotten of the man that so long ago attacked my mother.

Now, I had to find out if Bruno would hunt squirrels. I decided to change the way I would hunt squirrels. Instead of being stealthy and trying to sneak up on squirrels or waiting for them to come out of their holes, I would hunt by sight and run hard and fast toward the tree they were nearest to.

Bruno learned on the first squirrel to hunt by sight. I charged, running in the direction of the nearest tree of the first squirrel I saw. Bruno did the same. The squirrel climbed up the backside of the tree in an attempt to hide by using the tree as a sight barrier between us and him.

Bruno ran to the other side of the tree where he last saw the squirrel disappear. I would be quietly standing on the near side of the tree. Bruno would be on the opposite side of me, thrashing about in the leaves, trying to see the squirrel. This would cause the squirrel to quickly slide around to my side of the tree. I would shoot the squirrel immediately. Before I had Bruno, I stood on one side of the tree and would throw rocks or sticks to the other side of the tree in an attempt to cause the squirrel to slide around to my side of the tree. Sometimes it worked, most times it did not. After Bruno, it worked every time.

By charging the squirrels quickly, they were being forced up into a tree that usually was not their home tree. Therefore, they had no hole to hide in and were easy prey for Bruno and me. Sometimes we shot two or three squirrels in one tree. I went from getting a couple of squirrels per hunt to getting seven to ten squirrels per hunt. This was beginning to be a problem.

My dad had a rule, "You have to eat what you kill, unless it's a varmint."

Eating it was the easy part. The hard part was skinning and cleaning squirrels. It involves a lot of time and work. I would freeze the squirrels after cleaning them, and my mother would make delicious Brunswick stew in the winter.

She did not mind cooking as long as I did the cleaning. I thought that was a pretty good deal.

Hunting was beginning to cut into my egg grading time. I spent a considerable amount of time grading the eggs of 150 chickens. Each egg had to be weighed and candled. Weighing in grams determined if the egg was an extra-large, large, medium or small egg. That was a big deal because each size increase meant 10 cents more per dozen. My father hand-made a homemade candler, which was a wooden box, built 1-foot square with a light bulb attached inside and the opposite end left open (no board). A smooth circular hole was cut in the middle of one side.

The box resembled a bird box. I had Leghorn hens, which laid white eggs. The eggs would become translucent when held up into the hole while the light inside the box was turned on and the light in the egg room was turned off. I would quickly turn the egg 360 degrees while holding it snugly against the hole causing the yolk inside to rotate and allowing me to see any imperfections in the egg. Eggs with imperfections (mostly blood clots) were thrown away. This process was time consuming but greatly enhanced sales to housewives when word got out that I sold eggs that were not bloody.

This process would not work with brown eggs because the brown shell did not allow them to be translucent. I enjoyed grading eggs at night in the basement while listening to rock n roll music. I listened on a transistor radio that I had won by selling magazines for my high school. Some of my favorite songs were "Kicks" by Paul Revere and the Raiders, "Sunshine Superman" by Donovan, "Dirty Water" by the Standels, "Black is Black" by Los Bravos, any song sung by the Dave Clark Five, and "Paint it Black" by the Rolling Stones.

The last two times I went squirrel hunting, I killed 12 and 13 squirrels, respectively. That brought the total up to 68 squirrels for that season. The freezer was filling up. My mother said there were enough frozen squirrels for two years. I decided to retire from the squirrel hunting business, hunting had become *"too much squeeze for the juice."*

From now on, I would just hunt varmints. I could kill them and leave them for the buzzards to recycle. I was done with skinning, cleaning, and gutting.

A varmint was defined by my father as "any animal, wild or domesticated, that interferes with or costs the farm money."

In other words, it was an animal that does more harm than good. There was a long list. Wild dogs or stray dogs running loose from the town were number one. They would run in packs like wolves and kill chickens, pigs and even bring down baby calves. Groundhogs and rats were a close second, followed by foxes, raccoons, starlings and crows.

Rats were a particular problem. Our farm had been annexed into the city. It and the land around it were zoned industrial. My dad had remarked, "They can't buy me out, so they think they'll zone me out. We'll just wait them out. Land is like water. The bigger you build the dam to hold the land price down- the higher the land price will go once the dam breaks loose!"

Less than 100 yards from our farm, a corporation had put in a number of commercial grain bins. These attracted a huge number of rats. They would live over there until the owners of the bins would attempt to gas or poison the rats.

Rats, being very intelligent, would head for the hills. The hills of course, were our farm next door. They would come over in irregular waves. The closest barn we had to the grain company was my chicken house. They were easy to see there. When I saw a rat suddenly appear in the chicken house, I knew there would be a new supply down at the cow barns very soon.

I called my friend Frankie, and we would hunt them every weekend night for about a month until we had killed almost all of them. The cats would finish them off. Killing rats was more fun than hunting any other animal, varmint or otherwise.

7 POACHERS

Fall 1967

Whenever I went hunting or out at night on our farm, I always carried at least one gun. If I went out alone I brought my over and under. I balanced out the weight of the pistol on the other side of my hunting jacket with ammo. When I hunted with Frankie, I brought a shotgun and my over and under. He always carried his semi in a holster on his side and a shotgun or high-powered rifle, depending on what we were hunting.

Our farm was an unusually good place to hunt. We always had trouble with poachers. My dad and grandfather did not have time to investigate every shot they would hear on the other side of our farm or down in the woods.

I would see poachers quite often when I first started hunting squirrels. They would ignore me because I was just a boy of 13 years.

When I turned 16, I decided there was going to be a new sheriff on our farm. I would often observe a poacher at some distance away, walking in my direction. I would hide behind a tree or sit down in a hedgerow or lie in a dry ditch and pull some leaves over my body. I would wait until he would walk just past me. I would then suddenly display myself saying, "what's your name and why are you trespassing on my farm?"

They would turn around looking very startled. Their gun would be resting on their shoulder or being carried across their body resting in the crux of their elbow. I faced them straight on with the butt of my gun on my shoulder and my gun pointing down at the ground directly in front of me at a 20-degree angle. The gun would already be cocked or the safety off. My trigger finger was on the trigger guard. I only had to make one small motion to be in a firing position.

They would have to make several. They were already in the wrong in the eyes of the law.

I was not.

After the first year of confronting seven or eight poachers in this manner, I never saw any more. The word had gotten out. No more poaching on our farm!

I never had a single poacher answer my questions or for that matter say anything at all. They nervously turned and walked back in the direction they had come from without uttering a word. They constantly looked back over their shoulder every few seconds to see what I was doing as they walked away. I followed them from behind at a distance of about 30 feet—perfect shotgun range. Once I was in sight of our property line, I would stop at a tree and watch them until they had left our property. I never saw any of them again.

It was an unbelievable adrenaline rush. I always fantasized that the man who had attacked my mother or some bully from school would try to poach on our property. I bet he would not be so tough then. Of course, none of them ever showed up.

8 BASKETBALL, A.K.A. "THE LONG BALL"

1967

My favorite thing to do in life was *selling* eggs, fruits and vegetables.

I also sold magazine subscriptions to make money for my high school. I would win stuffed animals, transistor radios, and 6-foot-long stuffed snakes. I had won 70 stuffed animals during the last magazine sales campaign. All of them were given away. It was fun to fill my school locker up with stuffed animals. I would wait until a gaggle of girls would walk by. Nonchalantly, I would briskly open the door to my locker, causing a dozen or so stuffed animals to cascade down onto the floor. The girls would grab the stuffed animals while squealing loudly.

Phil, an upperclassman who had a locker next to mine, stood there witnessing the whole thing, and surprisingly exclaimed, "Damn boy, you've got game!" He and I had become friends over the past several years just by having lockers next to each other. Our outward appearances appeared to be the opposite of one another. He was quite the ladies' man. Inside, we were the same. He would tell everyone that the only one in school who had a bigger foot than him was me.

Upon sighting the stuffed animals, you would think that the girls had just found a cluster of pop bottles or something else of monetary value. Girls were an enigma to me. They were sure a lot of fun to observe. I really could not explain the attraction.

Before my egg business got bigger, I would augment my cash flow by collecting pop bottles. I would take them to the local gas station and cash them in at 2 cents each.

I knew where all the hot spots were to find pop bottles: anywhere there were work-camp-like locations such as logging camps, where houses were being built, and railroad rights-of-way. Also, ditches next to public roads leading in and out of trailer parks. It made no sense to me why poor people would throw money out of their windows. It would sicken me to find a broken bottle.

On my bicycle, I had one large metal basket on the front of the handlebars, two side baskets on either side of the rear tire, and another basket on top of the rear fender for a total of four baskets. Every Saturday morning, I would fill these baskets with eggs and produce to deliver door-to-door to regular customers in town. I would scope out the ditches on the side of the road for bottles to pick up later. On the way home I would fill the empty baskets with pop bottles.

My second-favorite thing to do was to play basketball.

The third was hunting and fishing.

Everything else, such as milking cows and going to high school, was like pulling weeds in the garden. They were just the things you did in life in order to be able to do the things you actually wanted to do.

Playing basketball was a euphoric experience for me.

The game combined hunting, territory, family and recreation all in one package. By combining all these things into one experience and adding adrenaline, I would become so hopped up that I would feel like a kangaroo.

Someone challenging me to a game of one-on-one for money would create an even bigger adrenaline rush.

I had even learned how to bottle up aggressive emotion and release it when desired on the basketball court.

Playing full-court basketball was a superb way to release the natural hostilities that would build up in my body. The rougher the game, the better I felt afterward, as if it were a type of therapy. It was a huge release.

Hunting was expressed in the game of basketball by stalking your prey. You would do this by playing a full-court press, man-to-man defense. Using the sideline (a fence row) as a barrier and a teammate (hunting companion), you could set a trap against the sideline for your opponent (prey), causing him to panic and throw the ball away or even into your waiting hands.

Playing basketball was all about territory and boundaries. This corresponds to farming (territory) and property rights (boundaries). Basketball was congruent with aggressively protecting your farmland, home (your team's basket) and your family (teammates). If an opposing player took a cheap shot at one of my teammates, I made him pay the next chance I got while playing defense.

Offense was the recreation part of the game of basketball. It was the mirror image of defense. I loved shooting the long ball, especially when I could catch the defense loafing. Playing offense in basketball equated to leaving one's property and going out onto someone else's property. You would respect their property just like you expected them to respect your property.

I'd rather block a shot or get a defensive rebound than shoot the ball. I got more satisfaction from passing the ball and getting an assist than shooting the ball myself.

I denied the basket to whomever I was guarding.

It did not matter to me who on the team scored, as long as we won the game.

In the big picture, basketball was like farming. Neither one was work if you had a passion for doing it.

9 WINTER

1967

The dividing line between summer and fall is not as clearly defined as the line between fall and winter.

You wake up one morning and at daybreak everything outside is covered in sparkly icy white. Winter has officially arrived. By noon, any plant that is not winter-hardy is lying flat on the ground.

Of course, plenty of warning had been given. All the weather reports, every year, give a countdown. You start to pay attention when they call for it to get down into the 30's. The first time the weatherman says there is a chance of light frost, you know there could be a hard freeze.

On the farm, you first hear that kind of forecast by breakfast time. That's when any extra hands that are available pick everything that is susceptible to freezing in the garden. It was a job most everyone tried to avoid.

I enjoyed picking big crops of anything in the garden. The best part about vegetables and fruits from the garden was how good they tasted.

Also, when there were bumper crops, I was allowed to sell the excess on my egg route that I delivered door-to-door every Saturday on my bicycle. I got to keep the money. I felt like I was the luckiest kid around because I always had money for whatever I wanted. Of course, I had bills to pay too. I had to buy my own school lunches, my clothes and chicken feed for my flock of 150 leghorn layers.

My wants were simple. Fishing equipment, ammo for hunting, and a large coin collection. Every now and then I would save up for big-ticket items such as a bike, a new varmint gun or a litter of pigs to raise into hogs.

First, I would pick all the tomatoes, including the green ones that weighed at least a third of a pound. For the winter, they would be stored on newspaper, in the basement, on a table. Every three days or so, they would be checked for red ones to be brought upstairs to eat. Rotten ones would be taken to the chickens. I seldom had any extra tomatoes to sell. We would eat them fresh and can the excess.

Second, I'd pick all the beans. We grew butter beans and string beans. My grandfather grew butter beans on long, skinny cedar poles that he would cut from our forest. He would look for forked cedars where the fork was no higher than your waist. He then cut the most crooked fork off. He cut it in such a way that the cut was parallel to the ground. Then the pole could be driven into the soft garden earth with a few licks from the sledgehammer. This beat digging holes and packing the ground around the holes making it unfriendly for root growth. Growing butter beans and Irish potatoes was his favorite hobby.

I would pick the string beans first. They were harder to pick because they were in rows close to the ground and you had to bend over. I picked the string beans that had "gone to seed" (dried) along with the tender, sweet green ones. The butter beans were picked in the same way. Later, in the house, we would shell all the dried string beans and cook them in with the green beans. They were known as "shelly beans" and added a different yummy taste dimension to the green beans. My mom said they were very healthy.

We shelled the dried butter beans separately and stored them to be used in casseroles in the winter.

By the time I got to the butter beans, if not before, my grandfather would come to lend me a hand. He was a lot of fun to work with. He always had something new about gardening to teach me. There were never many butter beans to pick because my grandfather kept them picked during the season. He and I would have races picking fruits and vegetables. He was 60 years older than I was, and when we raced he would consistently stay just ahead of me, laughing the whole time.

We almost always picked everything by the afternoon milking. If not, my grandfather would go and help my dad do the milking.

I got to keep on picking in the garden. It would be icy by morning. The song, "A Hazy Shade of Winter," by Simon and Garfunkel would come to mind. And spring planting would only be around five months away.

10 HARD WORK'S NOT EASY

December 1967

Christmas vacation from school was coming to an end. There were obviously going to be many snow days in January.

"Dad is not getting younger," my dad said sadly one morning during milking. "And I don't want you to milk cows before you go to school in the mornings because you'll be too tired to pay attention in class. I'm going to check down at the State (penitentiary) Farm and see if there are any promising parolees about to come out of jail. Of course, I want your help with the milking every afternoon including school days whether I can get a worker or not and some mornings if necessary."

That meant no after-school activities of any kind. I always wanted to play basketball. I had put up a goal on the outside of the barn above the walkway where the cows came into the barn to be milked. Whenever there was a 30-second lull in the milking operation, I would grab my basketball, dribble around the cow pies as if they were defenders, and shoot a layup. I would immediately go back to work before my dad could say anything.

Once he said, "If only your legs and feet were as quick and strong as your arms and hands."

But most times he looked annoyed. Once he said, "You can't make a living playing basketball, so why do you waste your time?"

There were several reasons. Basketball was the one sport that went with farming. You could play it indoors during winter when there was snow on the ground. The other three seasons, the days were long and there was always work or some other fun activity to do outdoors until dark. Even after milking, I could feel energy and strength in my body that needed to be released. It was also fun to be better at something besides work than other boys my age. I could not tell my dad these reasons. He would think it was some kind of sin to put "play" and fun above work.

When I would ask permission to take part in extracurricular activities after school, he would say, "*Work before play!*"

Of course, work was never finished on a farm.

I had started washing cow bags when I was 6. I thought I had gotten off easy because my Dad said he had started washing cow bags when he was 5. As the years went by, my dad would quickly move me up to more jobs and much harder jobs. Up until about a year ago, I would complain about how hard the work was.

His response was always the same. "*Hard work is not easy, dry bread is not greasy!*"

This 'conversation' went on for seven or eight years. It was as if we were having a two-sentence argument. This argument took me seven or eight years to figure out and understand.

I decided it was important for him to win that argument.

From that moment on, I never complained again about any work we were doing. And from that moment on, he never said to me even once, "Hard work is not easy, dry bread is not greasy!"

He won the argument, but I won in the game of life.

First, I did not have to hear that obnoxious old saying anymore.

Second, I became the roughest, toughest, most dependable worker he ever had. I was a mean, lean, cow-milking machine.

It happened immediately, like waving a wand.

It was instant karma.

I felt empowered.

The expression, "*Hard work's not easy, dry bread's not greasy,*" comes from the 1930s during the Great Depression. Back then, if you were only interested in taking the easy jobs or no jobs, then you might get only "dry bread."

However, if you were willing to do the hard jobs, you could probably afford to receive bread with grease on it.

"Greasy bread" was much preferred in the 1930s because people were on the verge of starvation and "greasy bread" had a lot more calories in it. When it was heated, it also tasted a lot better than "dry bread."

The grease on greasy bread could be any of the following: butter, bacon grease, lard, chicken fat. Anything that you could soak bread in in a frying pan. People would take what was available.

If there was any one saying that could sum up my dad's life philosophy, that was it.

11 BLIZZARDS AND DAIRY COWS

January 1968

It was the coldest, snowiest winter that I could remember in my 16 years of life. Christmas break from school had been anything but a vacation. When I was around 5, I remember snowdrifts on the north end of our house higher than my head.

My father and I were the only ones to show up for milking. He even told my grandfather to stay home. The chickens had almost stopped laying altogether. It seemed as though it took all the food they ate just to keep warm.

We were also the only ones to feed the heifers. We would feed them between milkings.

Heifers were young cows that had not calved yet. Once they calved ("freshened"), they would give milk. Besides the 100 milk cows to care for, we had 180 heifers to feed also. Most of the milk cows would stay in the loafing barns during heavy snows and blizzards. They would go out to the silage troughs just long enough to eat silage. They could always get all they hay they wanted to eat in the loafing barns. The youngest heifers or calves were kept in stalls in barns. The next oldest heifers had three fields to graze in. They also had a barn they could get into and be fed hay from. These two groups could be fed from barns that weren't too much trouble during snow blizzards.

The third group had the biggest heifers and was the largest group. They had multiple fields to graze from, stretching over 100 acres of land that adjoined my dad's property. This 100 acres consisted of multiple owners who wanted their land grazed so it would not grow up in brush and weeds. Cattle make great bush-hogs.

This group of cattle did not have a barn they could get into where they could be fed hay. So, whenever there was snow on the ground, hay had to be hauled out to the field where they were and scattered in such a way that they could all eat at once. That usually was not much of a problem with a little bit of snow. It just took time for loading, hauling, and unloading the hay.

However, when there is a blizzard going on so that snow is coming down parallel to the ground, it becomes quite a challenge. On top of that, add a 23-inch record snowfall.

We loaded the wagon with hay and started off to the far side of the farm.

My dad was driving the Super M tractor, the most powerful tractor we had. It was barely making it through the snow. It had no cab. I thought I had dressed warmly, but the snow and wind felt like they were blowing right through me. I was able to move the bales around in such a way that I could get down into a box with a bale on top. I was in good shape.

Halfway to the heifers' field was the tenant house. No one was living there. My dad had fired the last occupant for being drunk more than he was sober.

My dad stopped suddenly at the tenant house. He immediately went inside. I quickly followed. There was no heat in the tenant house. The good news was, there was also no wind and snow.

My dad said, "I had to get out of the wind for a little while because I've lost feeling in my ears."

I said, "I see an icicle hanging down from the back of one ear."

He reached up and rubbed it off. He never did gain back full feeling in that ear.

After about 15 minutes of "warming up" in the tenant house, we drove on through the blizzard.

We arrived on the side of the farm where the heifers were waiting. The only thing visible during and after a blizzard, in the pasture fields, would be large islands of wild blackberry thickets. The heifers would be standing on these, in an attempt to get away from the snow. Dad drove around each island that had heifers standing on them. As he drove around each island, I would throw pitchforks of hay to the heifers.

The drive back was cold and rough. There were no more bales of hay for me to use as a shield against the wind and snow.

If the kids in school had had to do what I did, I bet they would not have thought snow was so much fun. It took over 3 hours to get that job done. I was glad to get home to a warm house and eat a big meal.

My dad said, "*Always feed your animals before you feed yourself!*"

Growing fruits and vegetables was becoming more attractive all the time.

By the afternoon milking, the blizzard had started to diminish.

All the other dairy farmers kept the dry cows that were not being milked separate from the milking herd. My dad kept the dry cows with the milking herd. This way he would continue to bring them into the milk barn. He liked to personally feed them and check them over twice a day. Each cow had its own assigned place and its own assigned side, and they came into the barn in sequence. Each cow knew what place to go to when it came into the barn. Even the dumbest of animals can be trained with food. All the other farmers had numbers on their cows and only knew them by their numbers. My dad had personally named each cow and knew their mother's name and their grandmother's name! His all-time favorite cow was Blue Nose.

He would often remark to me, "Boy, isn't that the prettiest heifer you've ever seen?"

I would just nod my head. I always thought they looked the prettiest when they were sliced up into steaks, frozen and wrapped in cellophane. My favorite food was steak and hamburgers, and plenty of them.

It was just my dad and me doing the afternoon milking that day. There was a dry cow missing on one of the sides that afternoon.

After getting the last two sides in, my dad said, "Boy, I'm taking the tractor out into the woods near the silage troughs to look for Susan, and you finish milking the rest of the cows."

It was easy to finish up the milking, once the last two sides of cows were in and fed.

I was just finishing up and looking forward to a big supper in a warm house. My dad came into the barn and said, "I found Susan in the woods. She had a calf. She's down and can't get up. I'm afraid she's in bad shape. She has milk fever."

Milk fever is when a cow loses all motor functions from a deficiency of calcium in the brain caused by her udder becoming turgid with milk at the time she gives birth to a calf. In order for her body to produce that much milk, all the calcium available in the rest of her body suddenly goes into making milk. This always happens to the cows that produce the most milk.

"*A downer and a goner*" is what most dairy farmers would have said, but not my dad.

"Boy, I believe you and I can save her."

I knew it would be a long time before I ate supper. I was game. The adventure would make up for it. My dad had a pool of farming knowledge that he could pull from. This knowledge came from listening to stories and working with his father and uncles.

He hooked a tractor to a slide with a buck, a pin, and a chain.

A slide was a handy, functional, yet inexpensive way to move things around on a farm. It had no moving parts. It consisted of two runners, like a sled, with boards nailed flat on top of the runners. The slide stood only 6 to 8 inches off the ground.

Onto the slide we loaded two shovels, a pick, a digging bar, and a long, heavy rope. I rode on the drawbar of the tractor.

The good news was it had finally stopped snowing. But the wind was still blowing fiercely, so much so that little pieces of frozen snow would blow into my cheeks like sharp pieces of glass. Eventually, my cheeks went numb. It took about twenty minutes to get there.

The cow and calf both looked like they would not make it until morning. The calf was sprawled out behind Susan laying on top of the snow. Susan was also lying down but could still hold her head up. Afterbirth was still hanging out behind her and mostly frozen.

My dad and I shoveled the snow away beside the cow on the side next to her back.

We dug a trench near her back with the pick and digging bar. The ground was frozen over a foot deep so this took a while. The trench matched the length and height of the runner on the slide.

My dad pulled the slide up beside Susan, so that the runner fit snugly into the slot in the ground.

He then looped the rope under her front leg and back leg that were on her top side.

We both anchored on either end of the rope.

Then we pulled on the rope, while keeping it taut, in a see-saw fashion, thus "walking" her to the edge of the slide.

With one huge burst of energy, we both pulled simultaneously on the rope. Susan was rolled 180 degrees over onto the slide onto her other side

The calf was placed on the slide between her legs.

We drove her to a corner of the loafing barn and unloaded her the same way she was loaded. The calf looked weak and frail.

One of the teats on her udder was blue-ish purple in color.

My dad said, "Susan will be dead by morning from gangrene if we do not get penicillin into the infected teat."

My dad always kept plastic syringes and bottles of penicillin on hand. He also kept quart jars of calcium gluconate on hand.

Looking in his cows' medicine cabinet, he found a length of rubber hose with a needle attached to each end.

He took a nose holder and applied it to her nose. A nose holder looks like a giant pair of scissors that do not cut but instead have two large metal balls made into the "tips" (or ends) that fit snugly into a cows nose. The opposite end (handles) can be pulled by a rope that is looped through both handles to make for a very tight hold. A rope was attached to the other end, which he tied off snugly to her front leg, pulling her head sharply to one side.

Taking the hose and the needle, he inserted the needle into her jugular vein. He held the other end of the hose higher than her head. I took the quart of calcium gluconate out of a bucket of hot water that we had put it in to warm it up. Then, taking the needle, I stabbed it into the rubber top of the bottle, turning the bottle upside down. The contents of the bottle slowly dripped into the cow's jugular vein while I stood there holding the bottle up.

He got down on his knees near the rear end of the cow and began to hand-milk the bad teat. Puss and long, stringy, viscous looking facsimiles of milk began to pile up on the shaving floor of the barn. Once the teat was milked out, my dad inserted the plastic needle up the teat three or four inches and emptied it with a plunger into the teat's quarter.

Grasping the metal syringe, he gave her another shot of penicillin on the top of her back above her hip.

Meanwhile, the entire quart of calcium gluconate had dripped into Susan and I had taken the needle from her neck.

My dad released the nose hold.

"Get up, Susan!" he shouted, slapping her across the back with both arms.

Looking bewildered, she got up!

It reminded me of one of those TV shows where preachers make crippled people walk. Of course, this took a lot more work and was very real.

Straddling the calf with his legs and holding it up just behind its shoulders with his knees, and placing a healthy teat in the calf's mouth, he forced milk down the calf's throat. Pretty soon, she was nursing on her own and looking lively.

Another miracle.

"I think I'll name this calf, 'Snowflake,'" my dad said proudly. "I think she's going to lose both of her ears to frostbite."

She did.

"Other than that, she should be a good milk cow, just like her mother."

She grew into one, and was easily recognizable from a distance.

I felt like my dad and I had won a battle against nature. It was empowering. It did not bother me that we ate supper very late that night. My dad said, "*Always take care of your animals before you take care of yourself, and they will take care of you.*"

12 MY FAVORITE EX-CON

February 1968

It had taken my dad several more weeks to get a new farm worker for the tenant house.

We had part-time workers who would show up when they needed drinking money. But now that my grandfather was 77, we needed a dependable man on a daily basis.

My dad did not view ex-convicts as a threat or a problem. He viewed their alcoholism or other addictions as the problem. He never had any problems with sober ex-cons, no matter how violent the crime they had committed. However, he did not tolerate drinking on the job or coming to work drunk. He fired workers who did this on the spot. All these men had a deep respect for my father and grandfather. They always addressed my father as Mr. Smith. For those who were married, he always addressed their wives as Mrs. Most ex-cons quit the day their parole expired.

My second-favorite ex-con stayed on for a while after his parole expired. He eventually got a "big-paying job" in Nevada mining coal. He had been in prison for an assortment of crimes, from stealing cars to fighting. He was a strong, quick and powerful man with bright-red hair and sky-blue eyes. If he had more discipline, he could have been a running back in the NFL. Woe be to anyone who called him "Red" while he was drinking. His favorite thing to do was to "whip" two men at one time. I asked him once why he liked to fight. He said, "It's the one thing I always win at!"

Once, he did not. One morning when he came to milk cows, he had four finger-nail gash marks from his neck to his temple. I asked him if the woman who did that had steel nails. He said it felt that way.

"I was on top of two men on the ground and about to finish them off, when one of their girlfriends ripped my face from behind. I turned and punched her out. Then two men jumped me from behind, and I was lucky to get out of there alive."

Later my father mused, "Maybe looking in the mirror will help give him something to think about." The man was in his mid-20s. His wife was in her early 30s with seven children, some by an earlier relationship. She was a rough woman. He eventually died of black lung at age 53. His obituary stated that he had dozens of grandchildren and great-grandchildren. During afternoon milkings, he would always chide me, "If you work a little faster, we can finish the milking early and go home." My dad had built a tenant house for our full-time workers in the corner of the third field away from our house.

The tenant house was on the other side of the farm from our house. You had to drive past the alfalfa field and the cornfield to get to it. The third field was separated from the cornfield by a hedgerow. The third field was a pasture that was home to the heifers that were soon to be cows. There was a very large fourth field that extended to the railroad tracks beyond the third field. Dad had recently cleaned up and added that land to the third field for the heifers to graze. The RF&P Railroad owned this land and let my dad use it rent-free in exchange for cleaning it up.

My mother liked the distance between our house and the tenant house. It was far enough away that you could see people but not hear them, usually. Summer was at its zenith when the corn in the cornfield grew up high enough that you could no longer see the tenant house.

There was little warning that my dad had hired a new worker. He announced at breakfast that there would be a new worker milking cows that afternoon. He also said the man would be on parole and therefore he thought he would be a good worker. The warden had highly recommended him because he was so gentle with the State Farm's dairy herd. "What was he in for?" I inquired.

"Murder," my dad replied.

My mother blanched visibly.

"The warden said that he was a model prisoner"

"Why did he kill someone?" I asked.

"The warden said he was in a bar drinking and exchanged words with someone else and they got in a knife fight and Leslie won. He claimed self-defense and was convicted of second-degree murder and now he's out on good behavior after serving seven years. Also, he has a job to come to here, so I know he'll be grateful. Having a job to come to was part of the condition of his parole."

"Thank God we have guard dogs," said my mother.

We had three farm dogs that would let strangers pet them at the barn. If the same stranger came to the house, the dogs would attack as a pack unless called off by my mother. They were very protective of her and the yard around our house.

"Aren't you afraid of him?" I asked.

"No," my dad said, smiling. He was a bear of a man who had wrestled for the College of William and Mary. He seemed to be in his own element around the roughest of men.

"If you treat him decent, he'll treat you decent."

"If he comes to work drunk, I will fire him. And if that happens, he knows he'll go back to prison."

My father never shied away from aggressive men. On Saturday mornings, farmers would gather at the local Southern States to "pick up supplies." It was just an excuse to get together and talk and get away from their wives. One particular Saturday, the board of directors had hired a new manager for the store. He had recently graduated from the Virginia Polytechnic Institute (another college in Virginia that was a big rival at that time with William and Mary) and had been on the wrestling team. When he learned that my dad had wrestled for William and Mary, he predicted that VPI would easily beat William and Mary in wrestling that year. My dad disagreed. The argument became heated and escalated when the manager referred to my dad as an old man, whereupon my dad suggested that maybe they should have a preview of the two colleges playing each other by having a wrestling match themselves. The manager agreed. Everyone went to the Southern States warehouse and got numerous burlap bags to take the place of a wrestling mat and laid them out in a square. All the farmers gathered around the square. Someone whistled loudly and the match began. My dad pinned his opponent in under 10 seconds.

...

I was in a hurry to get to the milk barn that day after school to meet the new worker. I had imagined he would be some huge hulk of a guy. He was very normal-looking and appeared to be somewhat on the small side, but lithe and strong.

My dad introduced us and told Leslie that I would be showing him the ropes in the milk barn. My dad said he would be bringing the cattle into the barn and feeding them while Leslie and I did the milking. My dad was taking my grandfather's job and I was taking my dad's job and Leslie was taking my job.

Leslie smiled at me really big and shook my hand, vigorously saying, "Lead on, Brudder!"

I was taken aback by his friendliness. He had a sincerity about him that made me immediately like him.

At supper my mother asked, "How did the new man do?"

"He had no problem catching on and easily kept up with me," I said assuredly.

"He's quicker than a cat," my dad stated.

Leslie and I were such a good team that we'd finish the evening milking 30 minutes earlier than was typical. He was very pleasant to work with and had a great sense of humor. Toward the end of the week, he asked me if I would meet him an hour earlier than we were supposed to start milking on Sunday. He wanted me to write a letter for him. Since it was the middle of winter with nothing else to do and the milk room was heated, I agreed.

We met at the agreed-upon time. He told me that he had never learned to read or write. He wanted me to write a love letter for him to a woman in Richmond. I asked him if the woman could read or write. He said she was real smart and could do both. He had someone write her, for him, while he was in prison and she had written him back. My dad was giving him one paid weekend per month off and he was planning to take the bus to Richmond to see her.

"Little Brudder, I want youse to writes a letter exactly like I say it. Den I want you to reads it back to me."

"Okay," I said.

Juanita,

I gots out because I were good. Right now I has work yankin cow tits. I wants to git you down before Leon gits you down. I comes to see you Saturday 3 weeks.

Leslie

I read it to him. He smiled real big and said, "You think she likes it?"

"I think I would say the same thing, but word it differently?" I implored.

"Otay, writ it."

My dear Juanita,

I got out early on good behavior. I am working full-time on a dairy farm in Fredericksburg. I thought about you every day while I was away. I hope you thought about me.

I'm off from work the first weekend of every month. May I come and see you on Saturday, the 3rd of February for dinner? My bus will arrive in Richmond at ten in the morning.

Love, Leslie.

I read it to him.

"Dey teaches you to writ like dat in school?"

"Yes," I said.

"Dat's pretty talk. She'll like dat. Thanks, lil' Brother."

"Let's go feed the hay in the milk barn," I said, changing the topic, "before they come in to be milked."

"Okay."

I reached in my pocket for my knife to cut the strings on the bales of hay. I had left it at the house.

"Leslie, do you have a knife to cut the hay bale twine?"

He reached in his pocket, pulling out a long knife. Pressing a button on the side, it opened with a scary "Thunk!"

I instantly took a quick step back.

"Don't worry lil' Brother, you are real good to me."

He began to saw the twine with the knife, eventually cutting it.

"That's the dullest knife I've ever seen," I said surprisingly.

He looked at me smiling, "Dis knife is made for poking, not slicing." He demonstrated by touching the needlelike tip with his fingertip.

"Why?" I asked ignorantly.

"Slicing mens just make dems madder, but if you pokes da mens in da right spots- all you has to dos is jus' stay out of him's way till him's bleeds out."

I was glad we were friends.

"Have you been in a lot of knife fights?" I asked. I had observed over a dozen large, nasty-looking scars on his chest and back whenever he took his shirt off.

He just smiled and said, "Are dere older boys in your school dats are mean to youse?"

"Yes."

"Does you wants to git backs at dem and hurts dem likes dey hurts you? You is stronger den you look."

"No."

"Why not?" he responded, looking totally confused.

"Because they don't make me mad."

"Why?"

"Because in the big picture of life, they are just a bunch of losers."

"I never met anyone like yous lil' Brother. Other mens makes me mad all the time. Has you ever want to kill anyone ever?"

"Yes."

"Who?"

"The man that attacked my mother and got away."

"Tells me what happened."

After telling him the whole story, including what the attacker smelled like, Leslie says, "Dat's a very bad man. Now I know why your momma fears me. Not all black mens are like that. People talks, one day I finds dis man."

He had quit smiling.

...

Leslie came back from his weekend off with an extra bounce in his step.

"Lil' Brudder, you's the best letter writer I ever had."

"Are you going back next month?"

"No, hers was many good times, but when I ask her if I can buy some clothes or toys for her chils, she axe me to buys hers some white leather booties. Her's like my momma. She cares more about things then about her own chils. Lil' Brudder, yous has a good momma."

"What will you do on your next weekend off?"

"I stays in Fredericksburg and fins new womans. Maybe, I fins mans youse wants to kill."

Leslie was smiling big again with perfect white teeth.

13 SPRINGTIME IN THE RAPPAHANNOCK RIVER VALLEY

April 1968

It was the time of the year when my grandfather planted his garden. That was always one day in April- the exact day was different every year, but usually on a Saturday.

His garden, the early garden, (my father's garden was planted later, because it was the late garden), was on the far side of our 175-acre farm. The soil on that part of the farm was sandier – what we called "warm soil." My father's garden was planted later, because it was planted on clay soil which is referred to as "cold soil." This type of soil held moisture better and therefore could stand drought better than the sandy soil. This enabled our families to have vegetables continuously throughout the growing season.

Towards the end of the morning milking, my grandfather announced, "It feels like it's time to plant potatoes."

After breakfast, my dad went to town to buy pea seed and onion bulbs from Roxbury Mills. My grandfather went to a place in the old barn where we stored potatoes from the previous year's crop. We had been eating the Irish potatoes from there all winter. There were a few left. Some were rotten, others were shriveled, but some still had life left in them. These were recognizable by the little sprouts starting to protrude from the "eyes" on the potatoes. My grandfather took his pocket knife and sliced potatoes up in many different odd shaped pieces. Each separate piece had a "living eye" on it that was the beginning of a new potato plant that was to be planted in rows in his garden. I loved watching my grandfather take an old 'dead looking' potato and making the beginning of new life in the spring. It was like watching someone make a jigsaw puzzle in reverse. My grandfather was an expert at teaching farming with very few words.

My father got back from getting pea seed and onion bulbs from Roxbury at about the same time my grandfather and I had finished the potato sets.

My father had an old chisel plow that he had modified to be a row opener for planting in the garden. He had taken all the shanks off the front row, but had left 3 shanks across the back-row tool bar. The rows were spaced 42 inches apart. He would pull the old chisel plow and lay the rows off with an International M Tractor. For peas, he would just barely scratch the surface because he did not want to plant the peas too deep. Potatoes were planted the deepest and onion planting depth was somewhere in the middle. My dad liked to have wide rows (42 inches) because he would later cultivate between the rows with a mule. He enjoyed doing this as a hobby because it reminded him of his younger days. It was my job to lead the mule while he guided the cultivator.

I preferred tractors myself.

I enjoyed working in my grandfather's garden. The sensation of freshly plowed earth under your feet, along with the bouquet of fragrances emanating from the earth all around, was enough to overwhelm the senses. I felt like I was involved in some type of ancient secret ritual with my father and grandfather that had captured the essence of life. It was empowering and humbling all at the same time to have the honor of experiencing that springtime ceremony with my father and grandfather.

The garden area had been an old garbage dump and hog pen during the previous century. The garden was full of treasures from yesteryear. The best time to cultivate was right after a rain when the soil has started to dry out, forming a crust. I would help my dad put leather on the mule to pull the cultivator. I would lead the mule by the bridle between the rows of vegetables in the garden. The recent rain had washed the dirt away from objects that had been brought to the surface earlier by cultivation, exposing them to my gaze. Leading the mule, as I walked along I would be on constant lookout for marbles, arrowheads, Civil War bullets and old cork bottles. I would visualize these objects in silhouette in my mind as I was leading the mule or hoeing around the plants in the vegetable row where the cultivator did not go. This visualization helped me to more readily pick out specific shapes that I was interested in that were mixed in with pebbles and various debris on the surface of the garden. My favorite things to find were the arrowheads. It was hard to believe that once upon a time people made a living off those little pieces of pointed stone.

I was never paid in currency for working in the garden or anywhere else on the farm. But doing garden work, I felt like I was being paid twice. Each day while doing the work, I would find a pocketful or two of treasures. Also, my dad and grandfather would give me any extra vegetables we had over and above what our families could eat. I always had bumper crops of vegetables and strawberries to sell along with my eggs on my egg route in the Braehead Woods neighborhood.

One day, while taking a water break from gardening, I noticed an old well nearby. The sides of the well were made of stone and concrete. The top of the well had a steel plate bolted over it. I asked my father what the well was doing there in the middle of nowhere.

"During the last century it was also in the middle of nowhere," my dad replied. "There were two large plantation owners who did not like each other. One plantation owner owned land on both sides of the other plantation owner that he did not get along with. He also owned an easement that connected the two plantations in such a way that he could move a team of horses back and forth to work the land as needed. He dug this well by hand so he could water the teams of horses as they went from one plantation to the other. A pitcher pump was used to pump the water out of the well by hand into a trough for the horses to drink. When your grandfather and I bought the property, the wooden top to the well had mostly rotted, rendering the well a danger to passing animals and people. So, we bolted a steel plate over the well."

My dad went to his tractor where he always carried wrenches in his toolbox. He retrieved two wrenches and easily unscrewed the bolts, sliding the steel plate away, exposing the inside of the well.

"The stone work is really impressive on the sides of the well," I said. "And the water level in the well is closer to the surface than I thought it would be."

"The old timers knew what they were doing," my dad said with conviction.

Every so often, we would hit a rock in the garden with the chisel plow. My dad would dig it out and roll it over to the edge of the garden. I had noticed rocks on the edge of the field next to the garden as well. "How come the old timers did not get the rocks out of the field?" I asked politely.

"Nowadays, we work the land deeper than the old timers did, bringing up more rocks to the surface."

"Why do you work it deeper?" I inquired.

"This way we can make a deeper topsoil by mixing a lot of manure into the soil. We were able to do this because we have many more head of cattle than previous farmers before us on this land. The deeper the topsoil with more organic material in it, the better the water and nutrient holding ability of the soil. Hence, the bigger the yields.

Whenever my dad told stories about our farming ancestors, it was always with great reverence. He would explain how hard they worked to make something out of nothing. They would build the soil up by mixing any domesticated animal manure with leaves and twigs from the forest or weeds that they had pulled from their crops. Manure mixed with straw from the stalls made excellent composting material. They also would burn dead trees that they dragged into the fields which would add potash to the soil and raise the pH.

My grandfather and my dad were doing the same thing on our farm, but on a much larger scale. They were able to do this because they had several hundred head of cattle and three large chicken houses. Soil-building was achievable on our farm also because of the unusually good clay subsoil.

My grandfather's goal was to mold board plow all the fields on our farm at least once per year- twice per year if soil moisture was good. Each time he plowed, he would plow another half inch deeper than before. This would bring a half-inch of clay to the surface where it could be mixed with the existing topsoil plus several inches of manure and compost that my dad had added to the field with the manure spreader. He also took soil samples and always added the recommended amount of fertilizer and lime. On good years when he could afford it, he would double the recommended amount of fertilizer and lime.

When they had bought the farm, it had less than 2 inches of topsoil. Some places on knolls had no topsoil at all – just eroded subsoil. As a farm, it had been raped and pillaged.

My father and grandfather planned to create 18 inches of topsoil.

They were close to their goal.

They were making phenomenal yields of field corn, alfalfa and mixed hay per acre.

My dad was quick to point out that he and his father had huge advantages over their ancestors when it came to farming because of commercial fertilizer. They knew exactly how to mix the best of the old ways of farming with the best of the new ways of farming. They were an unusual team.

The 4-H motto came to mind, "make the best better."

I knew where I belonged.

14 BAREFOOT GREEN

April 1968

"I think It's time for the herring to be running," I said on the phone to my friend Frankie.

It was springtime in Virginia. The herring, shad, and white perch would be coming up from the Chesapeake Bay to spawn. The process had been repeating itself since the days of the Indians and before. When school teachers told the story about Squanto teaching the settlers how to plant corn by using fish as fertilizer; I knew it was springtime in Virginia and the herring were running up the Rappahannock River back in 16-hundred-whatever.

Frankie was the best friend anyone could have. He *really* had his priorities in order. Adventures, fishing and hunting first. Second and third were studying and school work. When there was an adventure pending, he would even come and help me finish whatever chores my dad had assigned me. My dad was quick to pay him one dollar an hour. Frankie's dad, being a doctor, seemed to resent that Frankie wanted to do farm work and would offer to give him money outright to do nothing.

Frankie took both.

We always had plenty of money for whatever we wanted to do. I sold eggs and vegetables. Frankie worked for my dad and had a generous allowance.

Today, we were going to invest in fishing gear. We rode our bikes about 3 miles into town to Barefoot Green's, our favorite tackle shop. We could only use our parents' cars when they were not using them. Barefoot Greens was conveniently located on the river on our way to our favorite fishing spot, the Power House.

Barefoot Green's was a one-story cinderblock building located on the

Rappahannock River in downtown Fredericksburg. It was owned and run by a man who was an expert fisherman, trapper and hunter. In fact, he was a living legend. My father's best friend and fellow farming buddy would come by on Sunday mornings and help 'milk cows.' They would take turns telling stories and reliving the old days during the 1930s when they were young men. To hear them talk, you would have thought it was the best of times. One of their favorite story topics was Barefoot Green.

There was a story about how he was so poor when he was a boy that he could not afford shoes and would go partially barefoot in the snow with a few animal skins wrapped around his feet while fur trapping to help support his younger siblings and parents.

There was another story about how he became the best professional boxer the Fredericksburg area had ever produced.

There were many stories about all his fishing accomplishments and his Native American ancestry.

Yes, he had attained immortality in the minds of my dad and all the other farmers in the area- *"a man among men."*

The Power House was a building that had been used to generate electricity many years previously. Water had been diverted from the Rappahannock River at an upstream location through a canal, which then deposited the water back into the river after turning the turbines in the powerhouse to produce electricity. There was a large concrete wall on the down-river side of the water exiting from the power plant. The wall was high and extended out to where the riverbank began. The fish, fooled by the false current, would congregate in a tightly packed area straight out from the concrete wall.

It did not take us long to get to the tackle shop.

"Frankie, do you think the fish will be biting today?"

Frankie responded, "Let's take blood worms and snag hooks as well, so we can't go wrong."

We rolled into Barefoot's and bought our usual one dozen each of blood worms, 1-ounce sinkers, and 3-pronged large snag hooks.

"Mr. Green, are the herring running yet?" I timidly asked.

"Yes," replied Mr. Green.

He was a man of few words. Only close associates and friends his age addressed him as "Barefoot." Each time I went to buy tackle, I always paused and studied the picture of him on the wall when he was a young man posing as a boxer. He looked scary. I would glance over at him after staring at the picture. He still had that stoic look he had in the picture, but I could tell that his eyes were smiling.

"Thanks, boys!" Mr. Green said, dismissing us from his store.

"Everett, lets ride past the Power House up to the Falmouth Bridge and see if there are people fishing yet," Frankie suggested.

"Sounds good," I said.

We enjoyed checking out all the cars parked along Sophia Street downtown, because most of the cars were from Maryland, Delaware and Pennsylvania. Fishermen would come down from up North because it would still be too cold for fish to spawn north of the Rappahannock River. You could not see the fishermen from the road because of the dense undergrowth on the flood plain between Sophia Street and the river. They were standing on the rocks or had waders on and were using artificial lures called 'shad spoons' to cast into the river.

"Everett, the fish must be really running because there are a lot of cars here today," Frankie said excitedly.

"Let's get to the Power House," I responded.

The opposite side of the channel from the concrete wall was lined with mostly locals. There were also a large number of fishermen on the concrete wall. There was a chain-link fence around the Power House. The fence was built so that it hung out past the concrete wall at a right angle over the water in an attempt to keep people from climbing around and fishing on a short length of concrete wall between the powerhouse and the chain link fence.

To Frankie, it seemed more like an invitation.

"Everett, let's climb around the fence to the other side," he said with a smile.

"You first," I said.

I tended to be more cautious, but thought it looked doable.

Frankie threw his pole, bucket and tackle over the fence onto the grass and effortlessly climbed around, going from link to link using only his arms. Looking at me and smiling, he baited his hook with a bloodworm. I threw my fishing gear over the fence and joined him, but it seemed to be more of an effort for me. By the time I got my hook baited, he had already caught a white perch. We caught half a dozen each in the next 30 minutes, and then nothing for the next half hour.

"Everett, no one else has caught any fish lately," sighed Frankie.

Some fishermen had already started to leave.

"I haven't seen anyone catch any shad or herring. I suppose they have spawning on their minds instead of eating," remarked Frankie.

"Let's wait till a few more leave from the wall," I replied.

A few more left and we went back the way we came. We replaced what was on our line with a snag hook tied about one foot up from the end of a line and a one ounce sinker tied on the end. We cast out across the river as far as we could. We then reeled the line in until there was no slack in the line and then jerked the pole back as far and as hard as we could. We would repeat this process until the line was reeled in or a fish had been snagged. Most every time we would get a fish on the first jerk.

"It's a good day, three fish and three casts," said Frankie.

"*They're as thick as hair on a dog's back*," I replied. "Let's show these Yankees (referring to any fisherman north of Virginia) how to catch fish."

I proceeded to add a second snag hook about a foot above the one already on the line. Frankie did likewise. It was quite impressive reeling in two large fish at a time in combinations of herring and shad on every cast or so. It was especially exciting when one or both fish were snagged by the tail end instead of the head end, because the fish could fight at least four times as hard. On my last cast, I hooked something BIG and strong. The line zigzagged crazily across the surface of the water.

"Frankie I've hooked a whale!"

"Jerk the pole again! Put the other hook into him!" yelled Frankie.

I jerked the pole again, instantly stabbing it with the second snag hook, whereupon the fishing pole snapped in half like a dried twig. I immediately grabbed the line, trying to pull it in by hand. The fishing line cut into my fingers, making them bleed. It was a lot like pulling wiregrass in the garden. With no hesitation, Frankie dropped his pole. Working silently, we eventually wrestled the line onto the shore. It looked like an unusually fat snake over 5 feet long. I placed my foot firmly just below where I judged its neck should be. It turned its head, exposing an open mouth turned toward my ankle as if to bite while thrashing the back of my leg with the rest of its snake-like body. I wasn't worried. My farm work shoes covered my ankles up about 8 inches. Seeing dozens of miniature sucker-like teeth in its rounded mouth, I exclaimed, "It's a lamprey eel!"

"They are bad!" exclaimed Frankie, "kill it!"

I pulled out my pocketknife and quickly cut off its head. All the men fishing nearby had gathered around. I had read stories in magazines how lampreys had swum in from the Atlantic Ocean via the Saint Lawrence Seaway into the Great Lakes and were eating all the game fish because they had no natural predators. I was thinking that I could be their predator if I could keep myself supplied with fishing poles. Five minutes later, the headless body was still thrashing around on the bank.

"Everett, cut open that eel and see what his last meal was," queried Frankie.

Placing both feet firmly on either end of the headless body, I proceeded to rip the carcass open with my pocketknife. Any farm boy *worth his salt* always carried a sharp pocketknife.

"Looks like eel roe."

"It is eel roe," I replied. "That's one female lamprey that won't spawn."

All the other fishermen seemed quite taken by the eel and our two 5-gallon buckets full of fish. Since our buckets were 90 percent full, we decided to call it a day.

We went to my house and cut all the roe out of all the female fish and froze it to be eaten during the winter with scrambled eggs. We also cleaned all the perch and shad and froze them as well. Some people would salt the herring down for the winter. Our family did not like salt fish. I fed all the herring to my 4-H pigs. We went to the barn and helped finish up the evening milking.

"How did you catch so many fish?" my dad said, looking at Frankie.

Frankie looked up from washing a cow bag, grinned at me saying, "The fish were not biting the hooks, so the hooks bit the fish."

15 YANKEES IN THE CORNFIELD

May 1968

My mother's mother told me stories about the War of Northern Aggression. Her ancestors in her grandparents' generation had ridden with Mosby's Raiders. Realizing she had personally known these people made it seem like not that long ago.

She told me how Gen. Robert E. Lee had given Mosby orders to get the best of the best horsemen out of the Confederate Calvary under Gen. J.E.B. Stuart. Around 20 of her ancestors on the Gibson side of the family had ridden with Mosby. By the end of the war, most had left Virginia for California. None of her ancestors had been killed or captured.

I never heard her tell anyone else these stories and she only told them to me when no one else was around. She always talked in a suppressed voice.

I asked her why it seemed that she was telling me a secret.

"Eavesdroppers and retribution," she replied. Eavesdroppers were people who back in the day would stand under eaves next to a window to listen in on conversations. The houses were built of thin clapboard and windows were always open during the summer because there was no such thing as air conditioning. During the War of Northern Aggression, it was sometimes hard to tell friend from foe. People were careful where they talked about politics. It was generally in the middle of a field and never in front of children or the help.

"Unbeknownst to most people, the Yankees occupied the South for 10 years after the war," my grandmother told me. "After Lee surrendered, the Yankees had the roster of all the names of the men that fought under Mosby. Mosby had inflicted much devastation, mostly financial, on the Yankees. Merchants who had lost wagon trains or train loads of goods to Mosby's raiders were out for revenge. Mosby's favorite things to take were horses, horse leather, Spencer's repeating rifles, six shooters, greenbacks, and gold. What they could not take, they burned in order to keep the Union soldiers from being supplied. Some of our ancestors changed their names or moved to California, and some of our family tombstones were removed to keep from revealing a family's home place"

She told me that before a raid, the raiders would make plans to meet up at a rendezvous spot later. After the raid, all the raiders would split up and escape in different directions and end up arriving at the gathering point from opposite ways. That way when the Union cavalry arrived to pick up the trail, it became close to impossible and nonproductive to follow a single horse trail. But sometimes, the trail was just clear enough that they could follow one or two horses.

Each raider would always double back to a vantage point to see if he was being followed. If so, he would then ride his horse along with the packhorse loaded with booty into a forest or near a cornfield.

Once in the forest, he would dismount from his horse. He would then spook both horses into a stampede hoping that he or a friendly Southern sympathizer would discover the horses later. Careful to conceal his footprints, he would then find a large tree to climb up into and hide. He would then wait out the Union cavalry until nightfall before going to the rendezvous point.

If there was no forest, he would ride his horse to the vicinity of a cornfield and spook both horses. He would conceal his footprints going into the cornfield. He would then hunker down in a swale near the middle of the cornfield where the corn and the weeds were the thickest and wait. Almost always, Yankees would pass by the cornfield. Sometimes they would form a scattered line and walk through the cornfield from one end to another in an attempt to flush the Confederate trooper out into the open. The raider would crouch down as if almost on all fours, alternating with lying down flat and slowly working his way through the line of Yankees without being seen. Once through the line, he would lie down again and wait until nightfall before going to the rendezvous point.

"That's an incredible story, and it should be told to other people."

"No!" said my grandmother firmly.

"But surely there is no longer any risk of retribution," I said.

"The less people know about you and your business, the better!"

"What is a polite response to someone who keeps asking specific questions about your business?" I inquired.

"Tell them it's *'layovers to catch meddlers.'* By the time they figure out that they are the 'meddler,' they won't ask any more questions" replied my grandmother.

I suddenly realized that being a trooper for Mosby's Raiders was not so alluring after all; in fact, it was a very dangerous occupation.

My father's side of the family's War of Northern Aggression story was even less glamorous. My grandmother's grandfather, Dr. Marcelus Ferdinan Smith, was a surgeon during the War. He believed that if he had been a regular solider; he would have been killed at Gettysburg. Instead he was operating on the wounded. His claim to fame was that he could saw a mangled limb off in less than 3 seconds.

Fast was better than slow.

My grandfather's grandfather was a courier for generals Long and Lee because of his horseback riding skills. While he was away, the Yankee army camped on Oak Grove Farm, which was his farm in Louisa County. The Yankee soldiers stole all the animals and any other food they could find. My grandfather's grandmother, Charlotte Austin Bronaugh Quisenberry was alone on the farm with only the company of one ex-slave who had stayed on in spite of the Emancipation Proclamation. After dark, a Yankee solider broke into the house and attacked her trying to get into her "preserve closet." That was code back in the day for a sexual assault.

He had her down on the floor. She was able to get one hand free and grab her large brass key ring, which had been attached to her waistband. Hitting him in the side of the head, she knocked him unconscious. Getting up quickly, she grabbed a large iron poker from the fireplace and beat him in the head repeatedly until she separated his brains from his skull.

It was a hanging offense per martial law if a Southern civilian killed a Yankee solider, even in self-defense.

She and the ex-slave wrapped him tightly in a sheet before rigor mortis set in. In the middle of the night, they dragged the dead solider out to the garden.

The soil in the garden was relatively soft and therefore much easier to dig into for a shallow grave. Also, they left the garden looking as though it had recently been tilled. So, the next day when his comrades came looking for him, nothing looked suspicious or out of place. They thought he had deserted in the middle of the night.

Soon after that incident, her husband John Strother Quisenberry was shot through the neck by a Yankee sniper while delivering orders from Gen. Lee to Gen. Long. He managed to stay in the saddle until he got to Gen. Long, preventing the Yankees from capturing Lee's orders. The slug missed his jugular vein and neck bone leaving him with a nasty flesh wound that never fully healed. For the rest of his life, every morning he would work a bandana through the wound dredging as much puss out as he could. There was no such thing as an antibiotic back in the day.

After returning home, he dug the body out of the garden and took it into his forest and buried it six feet deep.

I thought it was a good ending for a bad man.

16 WHISTLE PIGS

Summer 1968

Hunting for groundhogs—known to us as whistle pigs—by day was very different from hunting foxes at night. It was a visual game.

We set up on a knoll as close to the center of the field as possible. In your mind, you'd already have a mental map of where all the holes were located in the field.

Each person would take turns being the spotter and the shooter.

Frankie's dad had a very nice collection of high-powered rifles and unusually strong binoculars. His dad was a member of the local rod and gun club and had won several statewide competitions. He would let Frankie use his guns and equipment as long as we took proper care of them.

Frankie was a better shot than I was with a rifle and a scope. So, he would always get the first shot in case there were no others.

I was better with a shotgun, so I would get first shot when we were using shotguns.

Frankie would look though the scope of the rifle while I looked through the binoculars. The binoculars were much easier to maneuver and also stronger.

Groundhogs had excellent hearing and smelling skills but were weak on sight. We would not talk. We would communicate by sign language.

Many times a groundhog would just stick his nose out of the hole to see if he could smell a predator. You could see his nose clearly with the binoculars, but with the scope you could barely make out his nose if you knew it was there.

I would point out the hole and tell him to aim low in such a way that the bullet would scalp the hole, hitting the groundhog. Watching though the binoculars, I would see a geyser of blood shoot up from his head that you could not see with the scope of a gun. Frankie would look over at me, and I would just grin, and he knew he had scored a hit.

From the time I spotted the groundhog until he shot would take several minutes. He not only timed the shot between breaths, but also between heartbeats. He was much better at doing that then I was.

While all this was going on, all my senses were wide open. I would become very aware of everything around me. It was as if my brain was going 100 miles per hour while the rest of my body was forced to lay still. In my peripheral vision, I became aware of every moving thing around me, even insects crawling up blades of grass, or just flying by. The hair would rise up on the back of my neck. I would hear the sound of the rifle and then see the geyser of blood anywhere from 100 to 200 yards away a split second later. Everything around me appeared to be moving in slow motion while my brain was in fast-forward.

After the kill, the process would start all over again. My brain would slow down until I spotted the next groundhog.

Frankie became so good at the long shots that I decided he should take all those shots and I would just take the easy ones close in at 100 yards or less.

I knew how to put a smile on his face, and mine too.

17 LESLIE CHASED

August 1968

It was a hot summer night. My dad did not believe in air conditioning. It probably had something to do with the Great Depression.

We did have a large, whole-house attic fan. My dad turned it on just after sundown while mom opened one screened-in window per room. The fan was so powerful that it created a strong breeze in every room of the house. By 11 pm, give or take an hour, the house was comfortable for sleeping. My dad would get up around that time to go to the bathroom; he'd turn the fan off then.

The fan made a lot of noise. Once it was cut off, the night sounds of summer on Braehead Farm were a comfort to hear: many different insects, whippoorwills, owls and an occasional night shower, the sounds that allowed you to lie in tranquil repose.

There were also night sounds that raised different levels of alarm.

There was a stand of tall pines about 120 yards from our house. Within these pines, there were three chicken houses where I kept my egg-laying hens. There were also two brood houses where I hatched and raised ducks and guineas. Three-dozen adult guineas roosted in the tall pines that I had raised from keets. We were about two miles from town. The dirt road to our farm from the main road was a good half of a mile long, and was the only way into our farm. We were rather isolated.

When a car turned off the main road and came down the gravel driveway, the guineas would start a chorus of alarm cries. If a car drove past the right-angle turn to our house and proceeded on to the tenant house, the guineas calmed down.

If the car made the turn to come to our house, the dogs would start barking, joining in with the guineas. That would get the immediate attention of my dad. He was a light sleeper and was always up before 4 a.m. to milk the cows.

If a person entered the farm on foot, no alarms were raised until they came near the yard of our house. At that point, the dogs would become very aggressive.

Ever since the attack, my family had farm dogs. Bruno, mostly German Shepard with some hound features had switched over from hunting squirrels with me to hunting groundhogs. He was so efficient at stalking and killing groundhogs that it was rare to even see them anymore. Misa was a pure-bred German Shepard that someone had given my Dad. They wanted to get rid of her because she was the runt of the litter. She was only about one-third the size of a regular German Shepard. What she lacked in size she made up for with ferocity. The third and last dog was Shag. He was a stray that showed up one day. Shag adopted us as his family and appeared to be a mixture of all known dogs. The three of them were excellent guard dogs and performed as a pack. Misa was the boss.

The greatest alarm was if you heard a human voice you did not recognize near the house.

...

At first, all at once, we heard the dogs barking, immediately followed by the guineas. A voice in the distance was rapidly approaching.

"Mr. Smith, help! Mr. Smith, help!" the voice cried over and over.

My dad was already at my bedroom door dressed only in his boxer shorts with his double-barrel twelve gauge in his hand. "Boy! Get your shotgun! Watch by the front door, come out and help only if I get into trouble!"

He turned on the outside light and arrived at the middle of the yard at the same time Leslie did. I could hear the sound of many footsteps pounding down the gravel road. The three dogs had formed a line at the edge of the yard beside the driveway, and were barking madly. There appeared to be six or eight men in the group, one man in the front with the others behind him. It was hard to count the exact number in the dark. Leslie was standing behind my dad, with his left hand on my dad's left shoulder and his right hand on my dad's right shoulder. He alternated looking over my dad's left shoulder, and then his right at the mob that had gathered. Leslie resembled a groundhog peering out of his hole at a predator, then pulling his head back into the hole, and then looking out of the hole again to see if the predator had left yet. My dad had shouldered his weapon, pointing at the man in front. He commanded the dogs to stop barking. They continued with low growls and snarls, their hair standing straight up on their backs.

"Mr. Smith, we ain't gots no quarrels wid you. We wants da nigga behind you." the leader said.

"You need to leave while you still can." my father retorted.

The man who spoke looked at me standing behind the screen door and at the darkened windows of the house. I could feel the hair standing up on the back of my neck as well.

I was ready.

"Der are more of us den yous."

I noticed the man held a pipe and some of the others had rocks, but they seemed to be fading back.

"I believe the two barrels of this scatter gun would thin you out quickly. I start shooting when the first one of you throws something, or steps into this yard."

I noticed that the back of Leslie's shirt was soaked in blood. I heard my mother and without looking knew that she had her double-barrel 410 ready.

"Wes gonna lets you off dis time," said the leader haughtily as he disappeared into inky darkness.

"Y'all come back when you can stay longer," mocked my dad.

Everyone stood where they were for a few minutes. When my dad surmised that the mob was a few hundred feet down the road, he suddenly yelled out, "Sic 'em! Sic 'em! Sic 'em!"

The dogs left the yard in their direction like bats out of hell. Their paws hit the gravel at the first "Sic 'em."

It was almost time to start milking cows.

18 PARIS INN

August 1968

There were three basic categories of workers that my dad employed. The first was a main worker that lived on the farm in the tenant house. Besides a weekly wage, he and his family—if he had one—would receive all the milk they could drink, vegetables from the garden, their own chickens and chicken house, wood for the wood stove, and the tenant house rent-free.

They were allowed to take off the first weekend of each month with pay. On Sundays, the only work my dad and the workers would do was just the milkings.

"No work between milkings on Sundays," my dad would say, "But God made cows to be milked seven days a week twice a day."

The second category of workers was alcoholics. They would work for three or four weeks and then binge drink for several weeks after saving up their pay. They were basically part-time workers that my dad hoped would be on the job during peak work times, such as bailing hay and filling silos. They provided their own housing off-farm.

The third category was boys my age. They were friends of mine who wanted to make money or just wanted something to do other than studying or sitting around watching TV. Or, they were boys who would come by asking my dad for work for the same reasons as my friends. They lived within walking distance in a nearby subdivision.

Dugan's Bar and Restaurant downtown was a favorite hangout for white binge drinkers and drinkers in general who liked to brawl. I don't know why they had "Restaurant" in the name, since men went there mostly just to drink.

For blacks, it was the Paris Inn. My dad would often get a call sometime after midnight from one of his workers to be bailed out of jail. He would wait until 3:30 the next morning to bail him out and then take him straight to the milk barn to milk cows at 4 a.m. My dad was a strong believer in natural consequences.

One of the most pungent smells I've ever encountered was the scent of a man who's been drinking and fighting for several weeks, locked up in jail, and then brought directly to work without a bath. It was more overpowering and rank than the smell that came from any part of a cow. Once, one of the teenage boys my dad had hired seemed to be trying to hold back a gagging reflex. He told my dad, pointing to a cow, "Mr. Smith, I believe that heifer that just freshened needs to be 'cleaned out.'"

A heifer that had "freshened" had just started to lactate, and "cleaning out" meant removing the afterbirth that did not discharge on its own during calving.

My dad looked at him without smiling, and pointed to the man he just bailed out and said, "There's your heifer." My dad had a special talent for bringing bingers back to reality quickly and teenage boys into a binger's reality.

Leslie had gone straight to the barn after the mob chase and intervention by my dad.

By the time my dad and I got to the barn, Leslie had the first two sides of 15 cows each already in the barn, locked in their stanchions with hay and chop. He also had the milking machines put together and was standing at one end of the barn waiting for us.

He'd washed out his shirt by hand and put it back on.

My dad said nothing while giving him a stern look.

We milked the first side of cows in silence.

Leslie and I started on the second side while my dad let the first side of cows out of the barn. He then placed hay and chop at each stanchion and then went out in the barn lot to get the next 15 cows.

There were seven sides of cows to milk twice per day. Each cow was trained to know which side it belonged to and which stanchion to go into. That way every cow in the herd was checked on twice a day, which was very important during calving time. I knew every cow by number and some by name. My dad knew every cow by number and name. He had his favorites.

My father and I had our own cow memory palace.

When my dad was out of earshot, I asked Leslie, "how did you get that gash down the back of your head?"

He explained that for the past several months, on his weekend off, he had been hanging out at The Paris Inn. During World War II, The Paris Inn had been nicknamed "Little Chicago" because of all the killings that took place there. He would take fifty $1 bills and put them loosely in a paper bag, folding the top down and place it on the bar beside him while he was drinking. If a man would ask him what the bag was for, he would say, "nots for yous!" If a man looked in the bag without asking and asked him what the money was for, he would say, "to make a stupid nigga axe stupid questions!" If words escalated he would invite them outside to the parking lot for a knife fight. If a woman asked what the bag was for, he would say, "for a real good times with yous!"

"Did anyone ever call the police?" I asked incredulously.

"Nobodys calls white polices unless somebody's dead. By de times de police gets der, everbodys is gone and da bar owner saw nuttin."

"Everytimes I has drinks with womens, I axe about da problem yo momma had. Last nights when I drinks with dis woman I axe da usual. She says, `da mans you wants comin' dis way right now'."

The man said, "dats my woman dar."

"I's hands her da paper bag and says, `shes my womans now!'"

"Hims axe me to go outsides"

"I laughs and says, `ok!'"

"Hims walks bys car and quick-likes pulls out a pipe. Him and all hiz friends runs at me. I's turns to runs, dat's when he hits me wid da pipe, but I's quick and he only hits back skins of my head. Dat's when I runs real fast to yur house. Yur dad good to me always. Gives me job, house, and saves me from jail. Yous has good family. I knows dat man is da man dat wus bad to yo momma."

"How can you be sure?" I asked.

"I just knows. One days I catches him alones. I bet him not so tough alone!"

Could the man that was Leslie's archenemy really be the man that attacked my mother?

My great-great-grandmother's response to her attacker suddenly came to mind.

19 OPENING SILAGE FIELDS

Late August 1968

It was a hot day in late August, so hot that you felt like you risked suffocation with every breath. The ground was so dry that little puffs of red dust would drift up into the air as you walked or when a tractor drove by.

There was no noise except for the rhythmic sound of corn knives slicing through stalks of corn.

The man in front of me, just to my right, was bent over swinging the corn knife with one hand and cradling the cut stalks in the crook of his arm with his other hand. His movements were cat-like, quick and sure. Sweat had made a line from his head down the center of his back on his long-sleeve shirt.

I was similarly dressed—blue jeans, gloves, baseball cap and a long-sleeve shirt. This "uniform" acted as body armor against cuts from the sharp corn leaves and the burn of the scorching sun. The fact that it was so hot was a distant third concern. The main concern was the white "willy worms". I had already spotted several and had immediately stomped them into the red dust as if they were part of some communist conspiracy.

After milking cows that morning, my dad sharpened four corn knives. The corn knives were curved and very sharp, usually fluted pieces of steel with a wooden handle about eighteen inches long. They were so sharp I could have shaved the hair off my arm if I had had any to shave. After the War of Northern Aggression, it was commonplace for farmers to make several corn knives out of an old Confederate sword. Much to my delight, my grandfather had saved one Confederate sword from such a fate by buying it for a few dollars at a farm being auctioned off for back taxes.

Looking at me my dad said, "Watch out for the white willy worms. If they fall down your neck while you are cutting corn, they will emit an acid that will burn your skin, worse than a bee sting."

I was ready; I even had the top button of my shirt buttoned. So far it was me: 2; white willy worms: 0.

Later in life I would marvel at the way my dad could make the work seem easy compared to other threats that lurked in the field.

I was putting distance between myself and the two men to my rear left. However, to my dismay, the man in front of me was pulling away. I tried to step it up but at the age of 17, I just did not have enough muscle. Suddenly, the man in front of me stopped and turned around with a big grin.

"How yer making out der, Little Brudder?"

Being called "Little Brother" seemed like an upgrade. My dad and grandfather always referred to me as "little boy". Of course, my grandfather called my dad, "boy".

Pretending to be tough I said, "No problems here."

Laughing and pivoting to his left, he proceeded to cut the corn on my row. Meeting in the middle he looked at me with a big grin and says, "I's keeps you goings, Little Brother."

As if on cue, the two men behind me immediately stop working.

The white man squinted his eyes and says, "Hey boy, how many rows has we cut?"

They both seemed to have trouble counting past seven. I seemed to be the mathematician of the group.

I said, "We've only cut eight, and have the four rows that we are on to finish opening up this end of the field."

My father did not believe in wasting anything. "*Waste not, want not.*"

...

The silage-cutting "machinery train" was long and needed room to turn at each end of the field. So, between milkings, for three or four days, we would cut the corn by hand that would have normally gotten run over and pile it in armloads to be picked up by hand later and pushed into the silage cutter. After opening up the silage field it would be time to start cutting silage. First, we had to pick up all the piles of corn. We had already cut the corn with corn knives to provide a place large enough for a tractor (sometimes two tractors hooked together), a harvester and a wagon to turn at each end of the field. We also had to cut a two-row swath down the middle of the field and down both sides of the field. These "openings" allowed the machinery to drive on the two hand-cut rows while harvesting the next uncut row of corn. It had to be done this way because the forage harvester cut to the right side and behind the tractor. This allowed the tractor to drive on open ground without running over any of the corn.

When the harvester was running, it looked like some prehistoric beast devouring the corn. The harvester itself resembled a Brontosaurus being pulled backward by a tractor. The front head end of the Brontosaurus was hooked to a giant wagon while it had a continuous bright green stream (chopped up cornstalks) regurgitating continuously from its mouth, landing forcefully in the wagon.

Of all the jobs on the farm, this one was the only one I really despised. My father would drive the forage cutter across the end of the field while the four of us would pick up the piles of corn and attempt to ram and stuff the cornstalks into the forage cutter. This was trickier than it sounds. The forage harvester was designed to do five jobs at once. By placing the corn stalks in manually we were skipping the first two jobs. The first job was a sickle bar that cut the stalks of corn off a few inches above the ground. The second job was one set of gathering chains that ran continuously up an incline causing the cut corn to tilt away from the machine and lean on the corn in the row in front of it. In this manner, the bottoms of the stalks (butt end) were forced into the machine whereupon they were caught and crushed by a crimper, which turned on a rotating metal drum with crimping ridges forcing the corn into the cutter. The cutter cut it up into many small bite-size pieces for cows. Then the blower blew it up a pipe that curved into the direction of the wagon, depositing the silage into the wagon behind the harvester.

It was like trying out for the farm Olympics. You had to ram and stuff the corn while at the same time avoiding the sickle bar, the gathering chains and in the end not allow your hand(s) to be caught by the crimper. At the same time, the machine emitted an unbelievably deafening noise because all five processes were going on quickly and continuously. The cutter and the blower were the loudest. I tried to make up for my lack of size with determination. Everyone wore gloves but me. I preferred corn-leaf-scarred hands to getting one caught in the crimper and crushed. The glove could act as an extension of your own hand, placing your hand in effect a fraction of an inch closer to the crimper. I had heard of farm workers losing a hand this way. I also personally knew one boy this had happened to. His father was so devastated that he quit farming.

After completing one end of the field, we would go down one of the openings to the other end. My dad would cut a row of silage as we went along. He would stop the cutter at regular intervals and the four of us would pick up piles of corn that were in front of the cutter. We would pick the piles up a good distance in front of the tractor while the cutter ran stationary off of the power take-off. Then my father would drive the tractor forward with the power take-off running the cutter to cut the corn standing in the row. Once he caught up to the piles of corn, he would stop. Then the process would be repeated until we crossed to the other end of the 16-acre field.

Once we got to the other end, we would pick up the piles at that end.

Then, we would open up both sides of the field. This caused the 16-acre field to be made into two manageable blocks or "lands" that could be harvested in an efficient way with the size machinery that we had.

...

The other man behind me was leathery black and tough as nails. Leslie would say, *"He's so black, he's blue."* He claimed he was 52. My dad said he was closer to 72. None of the other workers nor my dad seemed to like him. I always liked him because he always tried to *carry his end of the stick*. Also, when no one else was around, he was always nice to me and would entertain me with one lie after another. His favorite lie was to brag on the wife or girlfriend he never had. He leaned to one side and spit a huge plug of jet-black tobacco out of his mostly toothless mouth. I first witnessed him spitting tobacco when I was 5. Having never seen anyone spit tobacco before, at that age, I thought black people's spit was black. He reloads with another big plug of tobacco. He then presses one finger against the side of his nostril and blows at length. He then repeats the process on the other side of this face. I understood why he did not have a girlfriend.

He gazes at me and says, "Everett, what's da rush? We have tils milking time to finish dis end of da field."

I said, "Let's surprise Dad by starting on the other end of the field by milking time."

Willy, the white man, blinked fitfully as if a sandstorm was in his eyes and cursed profusely. Davey, the black man, stared at me as if I were crazy.

Leslie said, "right on, Little Brudder!" and went back to cutting corn, along with me.

Davey ordered Willy back to work. Davey viewed himself as the boss of the operation. He took great pride that he was in charge of a white man and a white boy. None of that mattered to me, as long as the work got done. Leslie saw through it all and would laugh spontaneously at Davey. Davey thought Leslie was just happy to have him as the boss.

The day wore on and my mind began to drift to thoughts of cooler times. I thought about next spring and when the shad, herring and white perch would be coming up the Rappahannock River to spawn.

We got started on the other on the other end of the field before milking.

20 FALL

Early September 1968

It was that time of year when nature gave you short sneak-previews of the weather to come. One morning you would wake up needing to wear something more than just a T-shirt to milk cows in.

On an evening shortly after the sun went down, a stiff breeze would kick up that made you glad you had on a long-sleeve shirt. It was the end of the first week of school, the Friday after Labor Day. My dad was in a good mood. The corn started drying down earlier than normal because of the unusually hot, dry August.

That had enabled us to start cutting silage and filling the silos about 10 days earlier than normal this year. That meant that I was there to help before school started.

The corn was at the perfect stage for keeping in the silo. Not too wet (all green) and not too dry (all brown). It was brown up to and including the ear of corn, which had started to droop over. The corn plant was at the beginning of the "dent" stage of development. We had completely finished one field of corn and opened up the second field of corn by the time school had started.

My dad, Leslie, and the two bingers, had finished almost half of the second field. There was one "land" of corn next to Leslie's tenant house and one smaller "land" of corn near the middle of the field.

There was still plenty of corn to block the view of Leslie's house from ours.

It had been an excellent crop of corn. Both silos were heaping full of silage with plenty of corn left to stack outside in a mountainous pile.

A silo is a tall cylinder-shaped tower designed for moist storage. Filling it with heavy green silage forces all the air out. This leaves an airtight material that ferments and keeps all winter long. Silage makes excellent cattle feed because it's a perfect combination of grain (from the ear on the stalk) and cellulose (from the chopped-up stalk).

Many people confuse grain bins with silos. Short and wide grain bins are used for dry storage of just grain, while tall and skinny silos store moist fodder (chopped up corn stalks).

Silage keeps very well in a silo but not as well in a pile because of air pockets. Whenever there was a bumper crop, we fed the silage to the cows from the outside pile first. This would take the pressure off the hay supply. On dryer years when we could only fill two silos or less, we would feed the heifers hay and only the milk cows would get the silage. We had many barns to stockpile hay in and did so on rainy years when we had bumper crops of hay. My dad liked to have at least two years' worth of hay on hand.

"Boy, *hay is better than money in the bank*."

"Why?"

"Hay prices always go up dramatically on dry years. If you have extra hay, that's the time to sell it. Besides, cows can't eat money."

The weather was a lot cooler. We were at a good pausing point. With the cooler weather, the corn would not dry down too fast. It was a lot easier and faster to put silage in a pile than into a silo.

I knew we would come close to finishing cutting the silage corn over the weekend.

21 DOVE HUNTING

Friday afternoon, September 1968

My dad was not in a big hurry.

I knew the time was right.

Frankie was already on his way to our barn.

"Dad, may Frankie and I please dove hunt in the silage field this afternoon?"

I had to be careful to use correct grammar and ask politely or the answer would be no. He would correct my English severely if I lapsed into talking like the help.

He was not a big fan of dove hunting, however there was an unusually large number of dove this year available for harvest.

"Boy, you've earned an afternoon off, but make sure you clean all the dove you kill for your mother to cook. *Waste not, want not!*" He exclaimed.

He really *was* in a good mood!

Frankie arrived a few minutes later driving his parents' Barracuda. We had the weekend planned out: dove hunting in the afternoon, first supper at Hardee's after dark, and basketball at one of the outdoor courts in town. Afterwards, we would alternate between fox hunting (it was a full moon tonight with clear skies) and rat hunting. Second supper was around 10 p.m. at Service Town (a truck stop off 95 in Stafford County). Next we would ride the teenage car circuit in town, have a second fox and rat hunt, finally roll into bed by midnight and at 4 a.m. start milking cows and finish the day cutting silage.

Frankie and I set up to hunt dove apart from each other. He took up a position in the larger block of corn near Leslie's tenant house. I took up a position in the smaller block of corn. We were each one-fourth the distance from either end of the field concealed by the uncut corn. Our shotguns could cover 70 percent of the field.

He would shoot several dove as they flew overhead. The gunshot would then rouse a big flock of doves up out of the field where they had been eating corn and fly in my direction. I would take a few shots and then they would fly back toward Frankie, whereupon he had a turn. This went on for about 45 minutes before most of the doves caught on and flew off in an easterly direction.

I heard a loud piercing whistle.

While hunting, we communicated with each other by different whistles rather than our own voices, which would startle the game.

Whistling only seemed to make the game curious, especially groundhogs. They would stand up from grazing on their hind legs. This immediately made them visible in our rifle's scopes and also afforded us the best clean-kill shot—upper torso or head.

We had arranged ahead of time when one of us whistled to meet at the persimmon tree. The persimmon tree was in the hedgerow on the far side of the cornfield near Leslie's house. We knew that hedgerow and especially the area around the persimmon tree like the back of our hand.

It was one of our prime hunting areas. Groundhogs dug their burrows within the fence line, which had started to become a hedgerow. The hedgerow afforded the groundhogs a hiding place from predators. Foxes would re-dig the groundhog holes out even larger to make dens. Over the years, birds that had eaten fruit elsewhere would eventually light on the top wire on the fence and excrete fruit seed on the ground. There were crabapple trees, plum trees, cherry trees, and best of all, one very large and healthy persimmon tree. My father had encouraged the growth of these beneficial trees by cutting out the "weed" trees (i.e, hackberry and alanthus). The persimmon tree was close to the end of the hedgerow near Leslie's house. In early fall, if there was corn still in the corn field, we would hide in the corn field on nights that were clear with a full moon and wait for foxes to show up to eat persimmons. The moonlight would reflect off the tapetum in their eyes making the fox an easy shot. Foxes were at the top of the varmint list because they preyed severely on ducks and chickens. Raccoons, possums, and skunks would take refuge in these holes from time to time.

We considered all these animals, except for the skunks, to be varmints. Skunks were experts in catching newborn rats or mice and eating them. There was always something to hunt along the fence line. It was an ideal habitat for animals because there was always something there for them to eat. Also, there was a clover and grass field on one side of the hedgerow and corn on the other side. Hedgerows were also excellent for foraging honeybees. My dad had 14 hives of bees from which we harvested honey.

Originally, the hedgerow was just a fence line that my grandfather had laid out between the cultivated cornfield and pastureland to the east. The pastureland gradually dropped off to lower, wetter land, making it less desirable for cultivation but great for pasture.

At the very lowest point there was a wet-weather creek that water flowed in during rainy periods. On either side of this small creek was a small forest, which was also a good place to hunt quail and rabbits. On the other side of the creek the land rose up where we had another pasture. Then the land dropped off again whereupon another wet-weather stream was surrounded by yet another copse of woods. Beyond that last stream was a small pasture parallel to the RF&P railroad tracks. On the pasture side of the railroad the power lines were within easy shotgun range of the woods. While baling hay during the early summer, Frankie and I had noticed that the power lines were a favorite gathering place for dove.

There was only an hour or so of daylight left. We easily jogged over to the power line area within a few minutes.

The lines were loaded with dove.

After the first volley the dove would fly off and then come back and land on the wires again. They did not see us concealed in the woods. By the third volley the whole flock left the area. So we had decided to call it a day on dove hunting since we had shot all that we really wanted to clean.

Across the railroad tracks from the pasture and the power lines was the beginning of the edge of town. It was the black section of town and most of the houses had tin roofs. We were wading through the brush under the power lines, picking up the dead dove, when I noticed things were eerily quiet. In the past, when we were working on that side of the farm, we always heard children laughing and playing. I stopped and looked across the train tracks.

"Frankie, why are all those people looking out of their front doors and windows at us, and where are all the children?"

In an instant, I realized what had happened.

"Frankie, when we were shooting up in the air at the dove, the shotgun shot was raining down on those tin roofs across the tracks. It must have scared them."

"We've got all the dove we've shot, let's go!" said Frankie.

Suddenly, out of the corner of my eye, I saw a cop car with a flashing light coming down the street on the other side of the tracks.

People had come out of their houses and were pointing at us.

Two policemen got out with guns drawn.

"Don't move!" exclaimed the policeman nearest us.

I heard a freight train coming down the tracks, and fast.

One officer had his gun trained on us and the other was attempting to get through the brush on the other side of the tracks.

I realized the freight train would cut the cops off before they could cross the tracks.

I said one word to Frankie.

"Cornfield!"

We took off in a dead run. I cleared the fence separating the power line right-of-way from our field. I was in the woods in a matter of seconds. Looking back, I saw that the freight train had already shielded us from the police. Frankie was having trouble getting over the barbed-wire fence. I ran back and pushed the middle wire down with all my weight on one foot while pulling the top wire up with all my strength. This created a large enough space for him to get through. His hunting jacket pockets were full of dove, making him wider than normal.

We headed for the cornfield. We knew all the short cuts. We were running through places that rabbits couldn't go.

Cutting through the last copse of woods, I saw a grocery bag tied about head-height to the crotch of a tree near Leslie's house at his end of the pasture. I could tell by the expression on Frankie's face that he had seen it, too. In an instant, I knew in my mind why I had not seen the bag earlier. By taking the shortcut back we had traveled through a more brushy part of the woods. We would have normally gone around that area. The bag was not visible from the opposite side of the tree. Someone had intended to hide the bag there. With the police chasing us there was no time to investigate the bag then. We were almost to the cornfield and the police were nowhere in sight.

22 THE MYSTERY BAG

90 minutes later

Frankie and I entered from the end of the cornfield by Leslie's house near the persimmon tree. I ran down the center of the cornfield to a swale near the middle of the field. Frankie followed. This spot in the cornfield is where corn would not grow and would drown out on rainy years. On average to dry years the corn in the swale would be the thickest and tallest in the field. This year happened to be an average year. The corn was so dense that I had to drop the tractor transmission down one gear so that the forage harvester would not choke up because of too much corn entering the machine at one time.

We did not have long to wait.

I could just make out between the upright stalks of corn the bottom of the policeman's pants and shoes as he briskly walked by. From the knees up, I could not see anything of him nor he of me.

He had come from the direction of the opposite end of the cornfield, taking the path of least resistance through the woods.

The shortcut had paid off for us. He had no idea where we were.

The sun was setting.

At dusk, I heard my father bellow out in the distance, "Hey, boy! Hey, boy!"

My dads' voice would carry almost as far as Frankie's whistle. Frankie gave one large whistling blast to answer. We crossed the alfalfa field and proceeded in the direction of the milk barn to where my dad was standing with his hands on his hips.

As we approached him, he stared intently at the shotguns in our hands. Leslie was standing 10 or 12 feet behind him with a big grin on his face.

"I knew those cops were lying when they said that you two were shooting at people with high-powered rifles," my dad said in a disgusted voice.

"Where did the other one come from?" I asked.

"One walked up to the barn from the corn field, and the other drove in here in the squad car."

"What else did they say?" I asked.

"They wanted to know if I had seen two young men run by the barn. They said one was tall and skinny and was out-running the shorter, stockier one. I told them I had not, but that I would be on the lookout," my dad explained.

"Boy, do not do anymore hunting of any kind in view of those houses," ordered my dad.

"Yes, sir!" Frankie and I answered at the same time, obediently.

"Be sure to clean all the dove you killed and put them in the freezer before you go off tonight," my dad commanded.

"Yes, sir!"

We cleaned the dove in short order with Leslie's help.

"Da *man* was after Little Brudder today," Leslie said, laughing.

I told Leslie the whole story of the dove hunt. He was his usual jovial self, until I mentioned to him about the mystery bag being tied up into the tree. His countenance became very serious and drawn. He left abruptly.

...

Frankie and other kids in school thought my dad was very strict. He expected me to do farm work first before anything. There was no time for athletics in school.

He had a few basic rules: absolutely no drinking, no smoking, and no drugs. All you had to do was follow those rules and get all the work done. There was always a finish line that seemed easy to pass for me. I even had time to do my own farm projects. I had 150 laying hens, one-tenth of an acre of asparagus and my own strawberry patch. I had money to buy my own clothes, two school lunches each day, and money left over to save. I had just gotten my driver's license. My dad had a 1959 Chevy that I could use whenever I wanted to with farm gas to fill it up. I had no curfew. I had no desire to drink, smoke, or use drugs, and did not like being around anyone who did. I got my fill of all that from all the bingers and ex-convicts that worked for my dad. As long as I went by his basic rules, the only punishment was that of natural consequences. I thought I had a pretty good life and did not see my father as being strict at all, although he was rather authoritative. That did not bother me. Discipline was important to me because it was essential to the big-picture approach to life.

I felt like an old soul who was in a holding pattern until high school was over.

    We had finished cleaning the dove and it was time to eat supper. Frankie and I always ate at each other's houses. We considered whatever our mothers cooked for supper to be just a snack. By the time we finished supper it was dark. My dad was going to bed.

    Our day had just begun.

23 PERSIMMON TREES

Friday, Sept. 6, 1968, 8 p.m.

Foxes were sneaky, quick and smart. They loved killing and eating chickens, ducks and guineas. They also loved persimmons.

In early fall, persimmons would start to ripen and fall onto the ground. Foxes knew where all the persimmon trees were and would run a route at night going from tree to tree. Persimmons would ripen very gradually and fall off the tree over a period of several months. This would provide food for wildlife during the fall.

We knew where all the persimmon trees were as well. During the fall we would hunt foxes on the same night that we hunted rats.

There were three medium-sized persimmon trees in the barn lot and one large persimmon tree in the hedgerow near Leslie's house.

There were other persimmon trees on the farm, but they were either in a forest or near a thicket where visibility was poor, even on a night when the moon was full and the sky was clear.

After hunting rats relentlessly for an hour or less, we would switch off onto foxes.

We would hunt rats by creating panic.

Hunting foxes required stealth. There was an outhouse within shotgun range of the persimmon trees on the far side of the barn lot. On moonlit nights, we would sit quietly with our backs against the "shady side," the side of the outhouse that would cast a shadow on the night of a full moon. We would wait for no more than thirty minutes for a fox to appear. If none appeared, then we headed to the next location. Sometimes we saw their shadowy figures gliding briskly towards the persimmon trees. Or we saw the reflection from the tapetum in their eyes as their heads would move in the direction of the moon. They hardly ever made an audible sound. When there was more than one fox, we would both shoot simultaneously on the count of three. One of us would count out to three by touching the other one with his foot three times. Frankie would shoot the one on the left, and I the right.

Foxes were so quick that you would never have time to get a second shot off if there were more than two.

Once I had gotten lucky. There were three foxes. We each got one, and the third disappeared. We had walked down to inspect and collect our kill. A large pasture lay beyond the barn lot. I scanned the pasture with my flashlight. I saw the tapetum of the third fox about 100 yards out. Immediately, I switched my over and under onto .22 Magnum rifle, and aimed for the eyes. I never saw an eye reflection after I shot, making me think the fox had run off.

It was not moving when I shot, it had just been sitting there, waiting for its buddies.

He obviously thought that he was far enough away to be safe and I was certain I had missed.

I always told Leslie my hunting stories. Two days later, Leslie was walking in from the direction of the barn lot during the afternoon milking. He had a big grin on his face.

"Little Brudder, I saw da buzzards circlin'. I goes to see what's dead. You is a killin' machine. Yous shot da fox in da head."

My dad always said, *"Boy, don't shoot at anything you don't intend to kill, and always shoot to kill."*

After hunting the foxes in the barn lot, we would go over to the large persimmon tree on the other side of the cornfield where we cut silage. The tree stood alone within the hedgerow/fence line. The fence line separated the cornfield from the next pasture. It competed with no other trees for light, moisture, and nutrients. The tree also received extra fertilizer, lime and manure when the cornfield and pastures were fertilized. It was big, lush and loaded with persimmons.

Once the cornfield had been opened up, it was an excellent place to hunt foxes. However, after the corn was harvested, there was no cover to hide in within the pasture or the cornfield while hunting. Hiding within the hedgerow did not work well because it was hard to see around the base of the persimmon tree due to all the brush in the hedgerow. Also, the foxes would generally see or smell you before you would see them.

Once a dozen or so rows of corn had been chopped, a clear line of vision would be opened between the remaining corn and the hedgerow. The hiding place in the corn and the viewshed of the persimmon tree were perfect. This setup would last for less than a week before the corn would be chopped at a distance far enough from the hedgerow out of shotgun range. We generally only got one or two nights a year of hunting at this location.

We had struck out on foxes at the barn location, but not the rats. All the rat shooting and commotion had probably scared them off.

A second location was out of earshot of the barn lot. We had just set up when a pack of foxes showed up. We easily picked off one each.

It was only an hour and a half into the night. We had already killed two foxes and several dozen rats.

We would go to town, play a pick-up game of basketball, eat second supper and drive the loop. This would give the rats and foxes time to come back out again for the second hunt.

The night was young!

24 METES AND BOUNDS

Tuesday, Sept. 3 and Friday, Sept. 6, 1968

We had plenty to do before our second hunt of rats and foxes. The first order of business was to play three or more full-court basketball games. There were two main courts in the area. One was at Kenmore park downtown, and the other was at Brooks Park in Stafford County. They both had lights and three courts, each for different levels of skill. Until recently, I had only played at the intermediate court.

Teams were chosen and your team waited in line at your chosen court until a playing team lost and your team could take the losing team's place. Your team kept playing as long as your team kept winning. Every team wanted the best players, so they could continue to play all evening.

I had just started my growth spurt. Most boys my age were on the downhill side of their growth spurt. My dad had always told me the Smiths were late bloomers. They were about as tall as they would ever be. I had recently been chosen to play on the main court. I was, suddenly, as tall or taller than everyone else, and I liked to play defense. Most everyone else just wanted to shoot the ball.

There were many good players at our high school and surrounding counties. My school had a very good team, and most of the best players were in my class. I also knew players from surrounding counties through 4-H and 4-H camp, and also from playing on the courts across the Rappahannock River at Brooks Park in Stafford County.

Our farm had been annexed by the city, and was no longer in the county. This happened when I was 4 years old. So, all my life I had gone to city schools even though I was strongly involved in 4-H in the county. I thought I had the best of both worlds.

Socially, I did not fit in either group. Frankie was similar because he lived in the county but his father, being a doctor, could afford to pay tuition and send him to the city schools. Fredericksburg had the best schools in the area. Neither one of us took advantage of that. Frankie's parents were very disappointed with his grades. I aimed only to make C's. You could do that by just paying attention in class and studying for one hour in study hall. Apparently, my parents thought I was doing well to make C's. My dad was pleased, because I always got the work done on the farm.

Suddenly, I was interacting with boys outside of school who were as foreign to me as I was to them. Other than playing basketball and going to the same school, we lived in two completely different worlds. They seemed to spend all of their spare time playing pool, drinking, fighting, wenching, and watching TV.

My family did not even own a TV.

Being the high school jocks, they were front-and-center of all cool things that were happening. Through the interaction of basketball, I was in the unusual position of being a fly on the wall. I felt privileged to live life vicariously when listening to their stories. They could tell some doozies. Especially when it came to the wenching part, which I assumed was 99 percent lies.

My dad loved to say, *"A smart person always learns from the mistakes of others."* My grandfather and father were as quick to tell me stories of their failures in farming as they were of their successes. My dad would tell me not to be afraid of making mistakes because you always learn more from failure than success.

I was learning a lot. It was a one-way street. The jocks never asked me anything about what I was doing. That worked for me because I like keeping my cards close to my chest. I was certain that they could not relate to the good times Frankie and I were having. The gun aspect of it alone would have totally flipped them out. To them, snakes were probably scarier than lions. They were very content to be ignorant of me. Being a farmer was not considered to be cool. They thought everyone who lived in the surrounding counties were all hayseeds and rednecks. They would ask me derogatory questions like, "Is it fun pulling on cows' titties?"

"I would not know. We use machines to milk all of our cows." I replied. At that point, they would have very confused looks on their faces.

"How many cows does your dad have?"

"One hundred milk cows and 185 heifers." I replied.

Their look of confusion would be followed by a look of shock.

"Why don't you come out to my farm one day after school and I can show you how cows are milked?"

The smartest one said, "Does your dad have any old tractor batteries laying around that he does not want?"

"Probably."

"We'll be there Wednesday after school."

"Okay!"

I knew instantly what he really wanted. They did not have any money to speak of and lived hand-to-mouth. Two of them had a single mother as a parent. The smartest one had a car. He was adored by his mother and got money from her and worked an occasional odd job to support his car and buy gas. He'd already had his driver's license for over a year. They were all at least one year older than I was because they failed a grade at some point in grade school. They also thought they were smarter than I was because they made C's and an occasional B in easy classes.

I had more important things to do than study when I was in school. Sometimes, I would only get a D or even and F if I thought the teacher was an unreasonable person. I could always count on getting a B in art or an A in Phys Ed to balance out the D or F. I loved Phys Ed, all you had to do was hustle to get an A. It was also a real moneymaker. I kept three complete extra gym uniforms in my locker to rent out. If a student showed up to gym class without a uniform, he would get an automatic zero for that day. I would rent out uniforms for fifteen cents. Kids would get very angry and refer to me as a Jew. In 1967, such stereotypes and prejudices were common as a way to criticize entrepreneurs. I would take that description as a compliment. I was running a business, not a charity, nor a popularity contest and I certainly had no plans to run for office. This was my comic book money. The only place you could buy comic books in town was across the street from our high school at Mary Washington Hospital. Comic books always came in the first Monday of the month. I would sneak over to the hospital during my lunch break to buy them. I never got caught. Spiderman and Batman were my favorites, followed by the Fantastic Four, Superman and Iron Man. Every time I heard Leslie Gore sing *California Nights*, I thought of Batman. Leslie Gore was not only a singer but also an actress. Her character was Catwoman's sidekick, Pussycat, on TV's "Batman" show, which I would occasionally get to see at my grandmother's house. My dad thought comic books were a waste of time and money. I hid them in a piece of furniture in our house that had a false bottom.

25 USED BATTERIES

Wednesday, Sept. 4, and Friday, Sept. 6, 1968

My dad would store used, worn-out batteries on the outside wall of our milk barn. When he got up to ten or so, he would take them to the local junkyard and get 75 cents apiece for them. I was using the batteries as bait to introduce the jocks to my world. There were currently four worn-out batteries lying next to the barn.

They drove in about mid-way though the milking that Wednesday after school. They had already played a couple of basketball games downtown. I knew they were looking for hamburger and gas money. The first thing they noticed was the drink machine on one side of the barn.

"How cool is that, Everett's dad has his own drink machine!" They proceeded to buy several Pepsis apiece. They were excited because the drinks at our machine were 10 cents each. Downtown, they were 15 cents each. I did not have a heart to tell them that it was my drink machine. I had to beg my dad to let me buy the drink machine. Being a dairy farmer, he was a strong believer in only drinking milk. I sold a lot of drinks to my other set of friends from Stafford who played basketball at night in our barn loft in late winter/early spring. By that time, most of the hay that had been in the loft had been fed to the cows. That opened up the loft for basketball.

They stood at the end of the barn staring at the milking operation and Leslie in disbelief while drinking Pepsi-Colas.

I always enjoyed observing city people the first time they saw a full-blown, state-of-the-art milking operation. It's like seeing and hearing an animal assembly line on steroids. Visitors would take one step inside the barn and immediately stop. They would stare, trying to process everything. First would be the cadence of the milking machines. The sound would be as pronounced as a metronome with more of a swishing noise instead of a clicking noise. Next would be the smells. The main smell would be that of 30 cows confined in close quarters locked in stanchions. There were two lines of 15 cows each on either side of the barn with a walkway down the middle. Both lines had their butt ends facing inward to the middle of the barn with their heads locked in stanchions facing away from the barn middle towards the outside walls of the barn. Their heads would be over a manger where they would eat chop and hay. A gutter ran the length of the barn behind where each row of cows stood. Every few minutes one of the thirty cows would either poop or urinate about half of a 5-gallon bucket's worth with each occurrence. The gutters were filled about one-fourth full with shavings to help absorb moisture and cut down on manure and urine splatter. The middle of the barn where the cows stood also had a thin layer of shavings spread over the concrete floor for the same purpose. The stanchions were loosely fitted around the cows' necks with a short chain attached to a bolt embedded in the concrete floor and another short chain connected at the top of the stanchion to a length of metal beam. Once the stanchion was locked, a cow could not back out because of her large head, which would not fit through the stanchion until it was unlocked. The sound of the 30 stanchions clacking with their chains caused by the cows vigorously eating and moving their heads and necks about along with the noise of the milking machines and the strong smell of cattle would overwhelm the senses of the uninitiated.

They were eying Leslie suspiciously. He was staring at them and grinning like a Cheshire cat. I introduced them to my dad and Leslie. My dad just nodded. He had his poker face on, which was not a good sign. I was sure he knew who they all were by their last names. He knew *everybody* in town and the four-county area either personally or by what their last name was.

Leslie sauntered up close into their space saying, "Yous fellers are good to my man Everett?"

"Yeah." They all answered at once very nervously.

My dad had not bought pipelines for our dairy like all the other dairies in the area had. He obviously thought that it was a good job for me to carry the 5-gallon buckets to the milk room. Once in the milk room, you would have to lift the buckets and pour them into a large container that had a filter in the bottom. The milk would then flow through the filter into the refrigerated tank, which held more than 4 tons of milk. The milk was picked up every other day by a tractor-trailer truck. The milk buckets were solid stainless steel. A full bucket of milk weighed sixty or seventy pounds. I had two 5-gallon buckets of milk to carry out.

"Come with me to take the milk out." I said.

Eying the cows, they gingerly walked down the center of the barn, trying to avoid stepping on every speck of manure as if it were radioactive.

"Everett, why do cows shit all over their titties?" The dumbest one asked.

I pretended not to hear the question. I could see my dad out of the corner of my eye staring at him severely. My dad did not tolerate profanity.

I had carried a bucket of milk with each hand. To do this, I had to flex every muscle in my body, especially in my guts. Stand up very straight and breathe deeply. I only weighed 160 pounds. Once in the milk room, I set one bucket on the milk bench, the other on the concrete floor. The milk bench was about 15 inches off the floor. This gave the bucket-lifter 15 inches of less lifting to do. With one arm, I lifted the bucket by the handle to the height of the filter container which was chest-high. Then with the other hand I would tilt the bucket from the bottom so that the milk poured out slowly into the filtered container. I turned around and said, "Who wants to pour the other bucket?"

Everyone stared at me blankly. Finally the biggest one said, "No problem, I'll do it."

With both hands, he grabbed the bucket without using its handle by the sides of its top and placed it on the milk bench with much effort. After staring at it awhile, he attempted to lift it again the same way. He labored to get it up about waist-high, then set it down heavily sloshing some milk out onto the floor. He stepped off the milk bench without saying anything but looked rather embarrassed. I motioned with my hand for the others to try. They continued to stare blankly. Stepping up on the milk bench I picked the bucket up and poured it all in one motion.

"I'll stick to the basketball, you can pour milk." said the biggest guy rudely.

"I'll be doing both." I retorted.

Wasting time in the milk room had gotten me behind on the milking schedule. My dad had been feeding the cows from the manger side of the row of cattle. Leslie was caught up on washing the cow bags. As we came back into the barn from the milk room my dad said, *"Don't let your tongue paralyze your body!"*

His implication was that I was doing more talking than working.

I quickly took four milkers off and put four back on. My dad was still feeding the cows when someone asked me if they could go up into the loft to see my indoor basketball court.

"No!" My dad flatly stated.

To get to the loft one would have to walk in front of the cows to get to the ladder. A stranger doing this would scare the cows causing them to lurch backwards against the stanchion, which in turn would cause the milking machines to fall off the teats.

They had heard of my indoor court, but had never come to play, probably for several reasons. We only played half-court, the court was only wide enough for three-on-three, and it was not considered to be as cool as the outdoor courts. Also, it was well-known that my dad did not allow any drinking, smoking, or drugs.

Some of the players who played in the loft came from my high school, but most came from Stafford High School. Their parents loved my dad because he provided a safe place for their teenage boys to hang out on weekends, keeping them off the streets. We called it the Pearly Pavilion. It was named after Earl the Pearl Monroe. The loft was more personal, friendly, and private than the public courts. Also, during the winter it was out of the wind and the court never got snowed or rained on. I had become friends with the guys from Stafford County. I had been invited into their homes. I was quite surprised at all the things they had. It reminded me of the summer I had spent in Minnesota visiting my cousins.

I told my dad about all the things that my friends in Stafford had. My dad said, *"If a child is given everything, he won't appreciate what has been given to him."*

My dad would go on to explain how important it was to postpone instant rewards and gratification. His values and beliefs about farming had carried over into raising children. He believed in putting all farm profits back into the land instead of buying luxuries for himself and his family. That money would go into building up the soil and caring for the land. *"Always leave the land better than you found it,"* he would say reverently.

The guys had gone back to the area outside the barn next to the drink machine. The nicest guy, who was like a different person when he was away from the others, sang out, "Everett Mac, when are you comin' back!" referring to playing basketball at the courts downtown.

"Tonight!" I said in anticipation.

He and I sat beside each other in algebra class. He was the best ball player and all-around athlete of the bunch. I thought he was good enough to go pro. Whenever the teacher would leave the classroom, he and I would entertain the class by softly singing *Jimmy Mac* by Martha Reeves and the Vandellas. Recently, the teacher came back and caught us singing. He joined in and sang along with us. He was a pretty cool teacher, even if he was from Arkansas.

Suddenly, the smart one saw the four batteries next to the barn.

"Hey Everett, can I have these batteries?" the smart one asked.

"Sure!" I said.

I could feel my dad's eyes burning a hole in the back of my head. I knew he would not say anything then. Natural consequences would catch up to me later.

Chuckling profusely, the smart one loaded the batteries in his car. They all left without so much as a thank you.

"Why do you hang out with those punks?" asked my dad.

"I don't hang out with them." I stated.

"Why did you give them *my* batteries?"

"I felt sorry for them."

"Maybe you should be a preacher when you grow up so you can save all the punks in the world. Put 3 dollars by my place at the dinner table before you go to bed tonight." My dad said sternly.

My dad proceeded to release half of a barn of cows from their stanchions that I had finished milking. He then went out to the barn lot to let the next fifteen cows in to be milked.

As soon as my dad was out of earshot, Leslie laughed and said "Hehehe, Little Brudder is gonna be a preacher man when he growd up." We laughed heartily together. What a comical thought. Maybe I would get to meet Dusty Springfield. I had never seen a picture of her but I was definitely a fan of her song, "Son of a Preacher Man." I would lie in bed at night with my AM transistor radio tuned to the Cousin Brucie Show on WABC in New York City. I would listen to all the latest drug-oriented hippie rock music that I loved. My parents could not hear the music because I listened through an earphone.

Leslie had no idea who Dusty Springfield was, but he laughed along with me for the rest of the milking as if he did.

My dad was taken back by my friendship with Leslie.

I could not explain it. We had some type of chemistry. I completely trusted him.

I felt complete parity with him while working together. Neither one of us would try to put the work off on the other. We were a team.

"Little Brudder, you makes the job finish quicks."

"If I had to work wit dos boys, it would be like *trying to shovel cow shit with a spoon*," commented Leslie.

I had always wanted a brother.

26 DRUG-ORIENTED HIPPIE MUSIC

Friday, Sept. 6, 1968, 10 p.m.

The second order of business was to eat second supper. We had already done our first fox and rat hunt for the night and played three games of full-court basketball. We were always hungry.

In biology class, one of our assignments was to keep track of our food intake for one week and count the calories consumed. I averaged 5,500 calories per day—the most by far in the class. I was 17 years old, 6'2", and weighed 160 pounds. That was a big improvement from when I was 13. Then, I was 5'6" and weighed 99 pounds. My goal was to be 6'6" and weigh 200 pounds by my freshman year of college. I dreamed of playing basketball in college as a walk-on. The only person I told this to was my dad.

"Boy, there's no money in playing ball! Why would you even waste time thinking about it?"

"It's fun."

"You can't make a living having fun. I'm sure you'll be a big man that can lead workers. Besides, your grades aren't good enough to get you into college."

I knew I had scored well on tests, but I decided not to tell him that.

I figured that I would live farm life to its fullest right now. I would study and play basketball in college. I knew my dad had a lot of bills to pay. He had started buying land with his father as a partner in 1937. They had pieced together eight small tracts to make a 175-acre farm. Now, he was buying his own 100-acre farm about three miles away. We grew hay there for the dairy herd. He also had the use of another 100 acres that adjoined the 175 as pastureland for the heifers. Since I was 13, I had helped by paying all my own bills.

"I know you're not satisfied milking cows." My dad said sadly.

He was *right* about that.

"If you would spend as much time studying as you do playing basketball, you could make good enough grades to get into a good school and be a lawyer."

"Why would I want to be a lawyer?"

"Because they make money and you have a gift of gab that most people don't have and you're good at winning any argument."

I realized at that moment that my father must have a low opinion of me.

"Besides, you're more like your mother than like me."

I knew he did not mean *that* as a compliment, but I took it as one. After that, when people ask me what I was going to be when I grew up, I would mockingly say, "A lawyer." Some people would laugh, especially teachers in school and fellow classmates. In the real world, outside of school, my other friends, customers, and extended family members actually believed me. I was quite surprised. My dad seemed more pleased with me too.

I had my own plans and I decided to keep them to myself.

...

There was an unofficial route all the teenagers drove on Friday and Saturday nights. That included teenagers from the four adjoining counties.

The Quantico Marine Corps Base was only about 30 miles away. There were quite a few Marines there being trained for the Vietnam War. They would drive down and join in the route, too. The Marines would key-in on the local college, which was an all-girls school.

There were also the frat boys from UVA, who came to visit the college girls.

So, you had the townies, rednecks, jarheads, and frat boys. Mix them all together with about 2,000 college girls that were away from home for the first time, and you could count on some wild times and explosions. There was always a fight somewhere. The Marines seemed to show up in waves when they got leave from basic training. The locals and the frat boys were usually fighting each other. However, when packs of Marines would show up, they would all join forces and fight the Marines. It seemed as though it had become a rite of passage in our area to try to beat up Marines. None of it made any sense to me. Why would anybody fight over women? I had become an expert at avoiding fights. I knew how to vote with my feet. Whenever I saw trouble, I was gone. Some kids referred to me as a chicken. They would ask me whose side I was on.

"I'm on my family's side." I would respond.

They would stare at me strangely. Kids my age did not understand the big picture. However, it would be a different story if any of them came to my farm looking for trouble.

The best fighter in the world isn't bulletproof.

Part of that route included driving by the downtown Kenmore Park basketball courts. After that, we would go to a double-header location. On one corner was Hardee's, on the opposite corner was Carl's Frozen Custard. At Hardee's, I would buy the four biggest hamburgers they made, a milkshake, and sweet tea with lemon. Then, we would each get a quart-sized hot fudge Sundae with dried nuts from Carl's. I was the first person ever to order a quart-sized Sundae from that establishment.

The next place to go was Hot Shoppes across U.S. 1 from James Monroe High School. There was a waitress who worked there that went to high school in Stafford. We would go inside and order an A&W root beer float just to check her out. She was as close to a perfect physical specimen of a female that I had ever seen. We nick-named her Barbie Doll. Neither one of us had the nerve to talk to her.

The last, longest, and best part of the route was driving by and through Mary Washington College. It was a long sprawling campus, with a twisty, turning road going through its center. There was a good two miles of driving around it and through it. We never drove over the speed limit. There were a lot of sights to take in. I had never seen the campus at night until after we had gotten our driver's licenses. It was a very different place at night than during the day. These women made the girls in high school look like just girls. Apparently, there was no dress code in college.

My grandmother only lived a few blocks from the campus. She had gone to college there, and so had her three daughters. That was a long time ago. Like the song said, "The times they are a changing." My grandmother loved playing canasta, and was quite good at it. I would play with her periodically. The last time I played with her, she was lamenting how the college had lowered it standards. They were even talking about allowing men to go there! She went on to explain, that during her exercise walk through the neighborhood, she had observed several college girls with very short cut-off jeans filled with ratty holes and with a very small piece of material covering their "top". This left their whole midriff down to below their navel fully exposed for the world to see.

"What do you think when you see girls dressed this way?" She asked with a very stern look on her face.

"I don't know!" I answered with my best canasta face.

"What do you mean, you *don't* know?"

Continuing with my best canasta face I said, "Just as soon as I get a glimpse of those disgusting girls, I immediately avert my eyes."

She stared at me intently, continuing with her stern look. We continued playing cards for five minutes or so without saying anything. Suddenly she said, "A lot of people think you're crazy, but I happen to know that you are crazy, like a fox. Just remember Everett, *to enchant is to deceive.*"

I knew exactly what she meant, but sometimes it was fun to be enchanted.

It was very hard to beat her at canasta.

...

Some of the girls walking down the sidewalks of the college were the nearest things that I'd seen to the girls in the comic books I read. My favorite comic book girl was Spider Man's girlfriend. She seemed to be very exotic, especially with her red hair and the way she dressed. Her personality made her more like a real person than other comic book girls.

The first time I'd ever heard "Purple Haze," I was driving through the college. I had turned the radio up as loud as I could without blowing the speakers. There was a D.C. station, WPGC, that would occasionally play a hard-rock song. As soon as I heard the first few notes of "Purple Haze," chills ran up my spine. The hairs stood up on the back of my neck and I got goose bumps all over my arms. "The Sunshine of Your Love" by Cream affected me the same way. To make "Purple Haze" less druggie and more to my liking, I changed the lyrics from "'Scuse me while I kiss the sky" to "'Scuse me while I kiss the <u>earth</u>."

The guys on the public basketball courts were always talking about wenches and drugs. If drugs and wenches were more powerful than the adrenaline from playing basketball and hearing hard-rock music, then I didn't believe I could handle it. I decided that I would just stick to the music and basketball. I would never try drugs and I would admire college girls from the safety of my car.

Living life vicariously sure worked well for me.

When I first started driving through the college, the college girls would just ignore me. However, when I turned up the hard-rock music, they would definitely pay attention. That was when I first realized the power of drug-oriented hippie music. Some of those songs were, "Journey to the Center of the Mind," by Amboy Dukes, "Just Dropped In To See What Condition My Condition Was In," by First Edition, "Incense and Peppermints" by the Strawberry Alarm Clock, "Light My Fire," by the Doors and "That Acupulco Gold," by Rainy Daze.

Of course, the best song for driving through the campus was "Little Red Riding Hood," by Sam the Sham and The Pharaohs. The singer in that song was a wolf. When he let out a wolf howl in the song, we would let out a wolf howl of our own. Then we would start bleating like sheep. Other fun adrenaline-pumping songs were "Judy In Disguise" by John Fred and his Playboy Band, "Hello, I Love You" by The Doors, "Born to be Wild" by

Steppenwolf, "Bend Me, Shape Me" by the American Breed and "Time Has Come Today" by The Chambers Brothers.

To make the route complete, you would drive in the direction of the Kenmore basketball courts. One pass was enough for us.

There was a full moon.

It was time for us to go rat hunting and fox hunting again.

27 SERVICETOWN

Friday, Sept. 6, 1968, 11 p.m.

We drove back to our farm after driving the downtown route. It was only 11 p.m., and we were hoping to get two more hunts in tonight. Our farm dogs knew both of our cars and never barked at either one at night. This way, we could come and go at night without disturbing my parents. The dogs would stay in the yard unless I called them. I always left them in the yard at night because it was hard to know where they were in the dark while shooting rats. Also, they would scare off the foxes before we could get a shot.

We were hoping to get three hunts in tonight altogether. The weather was perfect: a full moon, clear skies, and crisp, cool fall weather. If there was a third hunt and we were still hungry, we would drive to the interstate and go to the next exit up north to Servicetown. By that time it was usually around midnight. My dad often reminded me, *"nothing good happens after midnight."* He was right. Most everyone left in town had been drinking heavily and was looking for a fight. Besides, Hardee's and Carl's were closed by then.

Going to Servicetown was like entering a different world. We never saw anyone we knew there. They were adults way past our age. It was as if we were invisible because we were only 17. We kept to ourselves. The food was good, plentiful and cheap. There was a lot of free entertainment while we ate. I knew from my dad's workers that it was a known prostitute hangout. No one I knew from school or anywhere else seemed to know that. Frankie and I were sure not going to tell them. We certainly were not going to let our parents know that we went to the truck stop. It was fun to watch the interaction between the truck drivers and the women. We could not decide who looked the roughest: the truck drivers or the women. What a contrast there was between the college girls and the women at the truck stop. The music was different there, too. We would almost always hear five songs we liked: "Ode to Billie Joe," "Snoopy vs. the Red Barron" and "Working in the Coal Mine" by Lee Dorsey, "Ghost Riders" and "Ringo" by Loren Green.

If we were not all that hungry, we stayed on the farm. We sat on 5-gallon buckets by the drink machine and listened to my transistor radio. We drank up some of the drink machine profits by knocking down half a dozen Mountain Dews each. We were addicted to Mountain Dews. We spent that time planning our greatest adventure of all, the trip of a lifetime. I was saving my money for a pickup truck, and Frankie would build a homemade camper to put on the back of the truck to sleep in. We thought we would be grown up enough to do it between our sophomore and junior years in college. We were planning a dot-to-dot-type trip. We would first drive to New Orleans, then to the Grand Canyon and hike down to the Colorado River and back up to the rim. After that, we'd drive up to Yosemite and drive up the West Coast to Oregon. On the way back to Virginia, we would stop in Minnesota to visit my cousins. We had been planning this trip ever since I came back from Minnesota several years ago.

Cousin Brucie would be playing some good music while we talked; "Sunshine Superman" by Donovan, "Devil with the Blue Dress On" by Mitch Ryder and the Detroit Wheels, "Good Vibrations" by the Beach Boys, "A Groovy Kind of Love" by The Mind Binders, "Somebody to Love" by Jefferson Airplane, "Brown Eyed Girl" by Van Morrison, "A Whiter Shade of Pale" by Procol Herum. We never could figure out what "A Whiter Shade of Pale" was about but it sounded so cool to listen too. Also, my two favorite songs that year: "We Ain't Got Nothing Yet" by the Blue Magoos and "I Had Too Much to Dream Last Night" by The Electric Prunes.

...

We started our second hunt down by the chicken houses. I had left the chicken house door open after the first hunt. This would allow me to quickly step into the chicken house with my gun on my shoulder ready to shoot with the flashlight on. Fumbling around trying to open a chicken house door at night while holding a gun and a flashlight would give the rats valuable seconds to scamper away. I stepped into the chicken house with my flashlight on and the butt of my gun on my shoulder. Frankie was at the main rat hole outside behind the chicken house. A fox was growling and running straight at me. It had apparently slipped into the chicken house just before me looking for a free chicken meal. I was standing between it and the only way out. The fox was cornered. My finger was already on the trigger. I pulled the trigger, shooting the fox point-blank in the head. He was nearly decapitated. I heard two pops from Frankie's .22 pistol. I saw no rats.

"I got two rats and you only got one?" asked Frankie.

"I bet you a 6-pack of Mountain Dews that I got the biggest one!" I said, laughing.

Neither one of us could believe it. We had already killed three foxes so far that night and several dozen rats. We had each killed our limit in dove that afternoon, played three games of basketball, eaten our fill of hamburgers, ice cream and Mountain Dews, we had driven the route downtown. Life was too exciting to sleep. We would catch up on sleep on weekday nights.

We usually hunted rats next in the granary, but we went to the persimmon trees in the barn lot instead. We were pumped up to get more foxes that night. We gave up after waiting 30 minutes and seeing nothing. Next, we were only able to kill three rats in the granary. We had really thinned them out. It was time to hide in the cornfield near our favorite persimmon tree for fox hunting.

28 NIGHT VISION

Midnight, Friday, Sept. 6, 1968

Hunting at night was a real rush. You would mostly lose your sense of sight. This caused your mind to reel in ways you would never experience otherwise. I sympathized with Hellen Keller. I could not imagine losing sight, hearing, and not being able to talk. You also could not talk because whatever you were hunting could hear you. We communicated by touch or sign language. You needed to stay next to each other. If somehow you were to lose sight of one another, the hunt would have to be temporarily called off until everyone was located. Nobody wanted to shoot their friend in the dark.

My dad always said, *"Only shoot when you're sure of what you're shooting at and then shoot to kill!"*

All your other senses would kick into high gear, especially your hearing. Nighttime on the farm was eerily quiet. It was a dramatic contrast to the daytime noises. There was at least 10 times less sound at night than during the day. But, your available senses were so keyed up, while night hunting, that any sounds you did hear seemed to be amplified tenfold. You could hear sounds way off in the distance. The furthest sounds were trains or airplanes, sounds that you ignored during the day. In the near distance, you would hear owls and whippoorwills. Closer in, the usual night farm noises prevailed: the occasional cow, guineas or dogs barking. You would even know which dog was barking. Very close by, you would hear different insects and know which ones they were. The snap of a twig or any new sound that did not fit in with the normal sounds would immediately catch your attention.

Smells at night are the next thing you would notice. You would know from which direction the breeze was coming, just by its smell. The horses and mules were in a different field than the cattle. They both had very different, distinctive smells. Those two smells were not offensive to me but probably would be to a non-farm person. The grain elevator, about 700 yards away, had a special smell, too, when grain was drying. It smelled like pop-corn popping.

The tenant house where Leslie lived in near the big persimmon tree had its own smell, like damp wood smoke, mixed with the scent of a person who did not bathe regularly. The chicken houses could also be smelled at a distance. That smell was an unpleasant ammonia scent mixed with a wet feather smell. If you were close to the chicken house or granary and they were infested with rats, you could smell them, too. The smell resembled that of putrid urine. The only good thing about rats was that they were fun to kill.

Whenever we hunted foxes at night, we always adjusted our stakeout position relative to the direction from which the breeze was drifting. Foxes had a keen sense of smell.

Fox hunting at the large persimmon tree near Leslie's house was next on our agenda. It was already past midnight. Frankie thought he should not push his luck staying out too late. His parents had not given him a curfew and he wanted to keep it that way. Also, he knew I was hoping he would help me cut silage the next day. My parents had not given me a curfew, either. My dad did expect me to be at the milk barn at 4 a.m. He had also made it clear that he preferred that I be somewhere on the farm if not in bed by midnight. I always parked the '59 Chevy where he could see it from his bedroom window. That way he knew I was on the farm, somewhere.

My parents had finished off a large room in our basement that I had recently moved into. The basement had its own separate entrance to the outside. That enabled me to come and go without disturbing my parents at night.

I decided that even though it was past midnight, I would go and hunt foxes on my own.

29 THE INTRUDER

12:30 a.m., Saturday, Sept. 7, 1968

I quietly slipped into the edge of the cornfield. Pausing briefly, I stood there with my body frozen perfectly still. I mentally settled in to become one with the night. I was focused on any and every sound and shadowy movement of any kind. I imagined what it must have been like to have been one of Mosby's Raiders on a moonlit night. Walking close to the edge of the corn to the other side of the field, I stepped into the standing corn, taking a 90-degree turn between the two outermost rows of corn. I walked gingerly between the rows in a crouching position. This enabled me to view the open area from under the ears of corn on the outside row. The bulk of the corn foliage that would have obstructed my view was above the ears of corn. Stopping occasionally, I would scan for any movement in the moon shadows and at the same time listen intently.

I was totally focused on a narrow piece of land 100 feet or so wide by 1,000 feet long. It was that part of the field that had already been cut and chopped by the forage harvester. It was between the rest of the cornfield that was still standing and the hedgerow where the persimmon tree was located.

Foxes were aware of the danger of being out in the open. They would access the persimmon tree by stealthily trotting towards the tree hugging either side of the hedgerow. They would not try to travel within the hedgerow because of its density. If they came up the cornfield side of the hedgerow, I could spot them at a distance. However, if they came up the other side of the hedgerow, on the pasture side, I would not be able to see them until they came over to the cornfield side of the hedgerow, to eat persimmons, if they came over at all.

I settled in between the corn rows on the up-breeze side of the persimmon tree, which put me much closer than normal to Leslie's house. I immediately observed that the light was on through Leslie's kitchen window. He was sitting at the table drinking a beer. That struck me as very odd. This was his weekend off. He never hung around the farm on his weekend off. He would always be somewhere else with a woman or drinking. It was already after midnight. Most Friday nights, I only got a few hours of sleep. Sometimes, if we hunted late, I would not even bother to go to bed. I would just go and start the milking a little early.

Frankie had already gone home to sleep after the second rat hunt. He did promise to help me cut and haul silage to the silage pile after breakfast as well as help with the evening milking on Saturday. We planned to play some basketball after milking and drive the route downtown. We would skip hunting and go to bed.

I thought back to yesterday afternoon when we were cleaning dove. Leslie's sudden change in demeanor when I mentioned the mystery bag tied to the tree was very abnormal.

I wondered what was going on.

Turning my acute attention to the persimmon tree, I strained my ears for any activity or unusual movement to the hedgerow opposite me.

Sometimes when different skulks of foxes collide under the same persimmon tree, they aggressively interact with each other by making low-sounding snarls and growls.

It was quieter than normal. There were no foxes about. I thought it odd. I had seen their scat around the farm and knew there was a big crop of foxes this year. I was about to call it a night.

Suddenly, I heard a branch snap, then the sound of feet scuffling as if to regain balance. The sound came from the other side of the hedgerow, directly across from where I was sitting in the edge of the cornfield.

The hair stood up on the back of my neck. Adrenaline pumped through my veins.

Whoever or whatever it was, it was moving toward Leslie's house.

I was staring intently, but could not see anything, nor could I hear any new sound or noise.

Leslie was still sitting at his kitchen table drinking beer.

The silhouette of a man's head appeared at the bottom corner of Leslie's window. He was looking inside.

Leslie must be warned. I did not know the intent of the intruder, but it couldn't be good.

All in one motion, crouching down as low as possible, I laid down my long gun and deftly sprinted out of the cornfield to the edge of the hedgerow. I continued down the cornfield side of the hedgerow, stopping at a spot in the hedgerow where we dumped various sized rocks that we found in the field while disking. I was there in a matter of seconds, observing that there were no other people on the other side of the hedgerow.

I was only about 50 feet from the intruder. I felt around in the rock pile until I found three rocks about half the size of a baseball.

A cloudbank swept over the moon.

I could still see the silhouette of the intruder peering into the window.

The hedgerow provided a physical shelter from the intruder.

Standing up, I estimated where the middle of his back was and threw one of the rocks hard enough to have crushed a rat. There was a short, sharp yelp from the direction of Leslie's window. As if already coiled, Leslie lunged away from the window to the opposite side of the room knocking over his chair as he went.

The kitchen went dark.

I was already running down the side of the hedgerow in a crouching position away from Leslie's house and the intruder. I knew of a small indentation about halfway down the hedgerow between Leslie's house and the persimmon tree. I was afraid that if I tried to run across the open area between the hedgerow and the cornfield, the intruder would see me, especially if the moon came back out from the cloud cover. I got to the indentation just in time. The cloud cover faded from the moon. I saw a black man standing about 10 feet from me on the other side of the hedgerow in the direction of Leslie's house. The breeze changed direction, and simultaneously an overpowering smell similar to silage liquor mixed with the smell of gasoline struck me in the nose like a fist. Memories of the attack on my mother flooded my brain.

Could the intruder really be him?

His body was turned staring down the hedgerow in my direction. I must not have been as quiet running down the side of the hedgerow as I had thought.

The moon disappeared behind a cloud once more, but not before I glimpsed the faint outline of a man stealthily coming from the direction of Leslie's house toward the intruder.

I was on my knees in the indentation of the hedgerow facing the pasture with my back to the cornfield. Had I been spotted? Maybe he could smell me? I had certainly sweated enough that day. Realizing I was downwind from him, he probably could not smell me. I lobbed the second rock down the hedgerow in such a way that it landed in the middle of the hedgerow about 50 feet away, making a loud rustling noise. Immediately, I heard the intruder move past me toward the noise the rock had made. Seconds later, another man appeared on the opposite side of the hedgerow beside me. He smelled of beer. I knew it was Leslie. He never acknowledged my presence or even looked in my direction. Leslie was completely fixated on the man who had run past me and now had stopped about 30 feet from me down the hedgerow. Leslie started to slowly move toward the intruder like a lion stalking a wildebeest. I thought I saw a silhouette of a knife in his hand.

The moon had revealed itself once more.

30 CLOUD COVER

30 minutes later

Leslie froze, leaning in toward the hedgerow. The intruder was standing down from the hedgerow, away from Leslie's and my direction. I threw the final rock so that it crashed through the middle of the hedgerow about 100 feet away in the direction of the persimmon tree. Out of rocks and not knowing what would happen next, I drew my .38. I figured one slug to the middle of the chest should do it.

The intruder moved away from me in the direction of where the rock landed. Leslie was moving in behind and closing in fast on the intruder.

The moon vanished behind the clouds.

I could no longer see them. I stood up, straining to hear any sound.

Thunk!

Someone shrieked.

I had bulldozed my way through the hedgerow and climbed over the fence to the other side and was moving towards the sound of the fracas.

I kept hearing a thunk, followed by a piercing shriek and then Leslie yelling out his own name.

The shrieks stopped. Now I only heard the thunk and Leslie yelling out his own name.

The moon reappeared.

I was standing next to Leslie. He had each knee pressing down hard on the back of the thighs of the intruder who was face down on the ground. Leslie stopped stabbing and yelling.

He said, "Dat's da mans dat was bad to yo momma and is da nigga I hates!"

"Is he still alive?"

"Hims' done bled out like a stuck pig. I firsts stabs him hard from behinds and aboves and twints the shoulders and cuts his backbone. Him falls like a sack of potatoes. The rest of the stabs wus fer funs. I yells my name so da nigga knows who's gots him."

I kicked the intruder's head with my work boot. It wobbled back and forth like a bobble head on the dashboard of a car. I put the .38 back into my hunting jacket.

Leslie rolled the body over, face-up. I immediately recognized his face from long ago as my mother's attacker.

Leslie was looking around wildly as if expecting more of the intruder's gang to show up. I assured him there was no one else about and if there was, we would have already known it. I walked the short distance to the cornfield to retrieve my long gun, just in case. Leslie walked along beside me, explaining how he knew the intruder was coming that night.

While we were cleaning dove the past afternoon, I had mentioned my curiosity about a bag tied up in a tree. Leslie said that upon hearing that, he immediately went to the tree and retrieved the folded-up bag that was tied to the tree. He found a large switchblade inside. He carefully replaced the knife and tied it back into the crotch just as he found it. Leslie said the intruder and himself had a blood feud going on that had escalated through trash talk and fighting over women. He was the same man that, with his gang, had chased Leslie and put a deep gash in the back of his head with a pipe. He had also bragged around the Paris Inn that the police were not smart enough to catch him for the assault on my mother.

"What's we's gonna do?"

"I guess we'll call the police and say it was self-defense," I said without thinking.

"No! Little Brudder! No!"

He explained that the police were on to their feud and were watching the intruder's gang. He knew that the intruder had tied the bag up in the tree during the day, when the police were not watching, to be retrieved later that night. If anyone with a felony record was caught with a gun or a switchblade knife they would go back to jail. That's why anytime the police were spotted coming into the Paris Inn, most everyone would drop their knives or guns on the floor and kick them towards the wall away from their table. The police would pick up the knives and guns and take them to headquarters. So, if he had been stopped by the police on the way to Leslie's house at night, the police would not have found a switchblade.

Leslie also explained it would be hard to claim self-defense when the victim had a dozen or so stab wounds in his back. Plus, he had already served seven years and gotten out on good behavior for second-degree murder. He was now on parole and could go back to prison, just for possession of a switchblade.

"We's gots to hide the body! I's not go backs to prison!"

My brain was going a mile a minute.

31 LESLIE'S DAY OFF

5 minutes later

My mind went back to last spring, when we were planting potatoes with my grandfather in his garden. He had told me about the abandoned well next to his garden that he had bolted shut with a steel plate. I also remembered the large rocks that he had retrieved from his garden. He had lined the rocks up on the fence line beside the garden near the well.

I recalled last winter's blizzard when my dad and I brought the downed cow and calf into the safety of the barn using just a wooden slide pulled by a tractor.

"Leslie, I know what to do."

"I knew yous would. You're smarts, Little Brother, real smarts. *Two heads are better dan ones even if ones is da hat rack*," said Leslie.

We took off in a trot toward the barn lot where the tractor and slide were located. We hooked them up and drove down the edge of the hedgerow toward the body. The top of the slide was only about 8 inches off the ground.

Leslie easily rolled the body onto the slide.

We drove the tractor and slide to the other side of the farm to where the well was located next to my grandfather's garden. While at the barn, I had placed a partial spool of smooth fencing wire on the slide. I instructed Leslie to bring some of the large rocks over from the fence line over to the slide, then to place a number of rocks on the body's chest and stomach area and wrap them tightly with the smooth wire, tying it as tightly as possible.

I got several wrenches from the toolbox of the tractor and worked three of the four bolts loose from the steel plate that was covering the well. I slid the plate to one side of the well using the fourth bolt that was still attached as a pivot point.

Meanwhile, Leslie had cocooned the whole body, including the legs and arms and rocks, with the smooth wire, tightly.

Leslie lifted up the head end of the body as I lifted up the feet and dropped it into the well.

Splash!

We looked down the well with a flashlight. We could see nothing but water. We bolted the plate back exactly the way we found it. We sat next to each other on the edge of the slide in silence for about 20 minutes. I felt a great sense of satisfaction knowing we had killed my mother's attacker. To me it was no different than killing a rat. I knew Leslie was a stone-cold killer but that did not bother me. I felt no fear of him, and knew he would do anything for me.

"Little Brudder, we's makes a good team." Leslie said with conviction. "It's almost times to milk. I's helps you's milk cows today."

I explained to him if he came to work on his one weekend off in a month that my dad would be very perplexed. The best thing he could do would be to get cleaned up, don't drink any more beer, and go to bed. Then, come to work Monday at 4 a.m. as if nothing had happened. I would go now and get the milking started by myself since it was almost time to start anyway.

I had already milked the first half of the first side of cows when my dad came down to the barn at 4 a.m.

"Busy night?"

"Very." I responded quickly. "After we got our limit on dove, we killed dozens of rats and three foxes."

"This is Leslie's weekend off, is Frankie coming over to help us cut silage?"

"Yes sir!"

My dad had a unique way of communicating; I always knew he heard what I said even if he did not respond to me verbally. I could tell by the expression on his face, or he would bring it up later when it fit into his conversation. When working, he always kept the conversation on task.

Leslie and I knew we could never tell anyone what had happened, not even Frankie.

32 RYE BEHIND CORN

Saturday, Sept. 7 – Monday, Sept. 9, 1968

My dad, Frankie, the two bingers and I cut silage between the two milkings. We got a lot done. I thought we could finish Sunday, before Leslie came back to work on Monday.

I was exhausted and went to bed after super. Frankie went home and did the same.

Leslie came in punctually at 4 a.m. Monday morning to milk cows. He and my dad were talking in the milk room. Leslie came back from the milk room looking rather somber. Leslie explained to me that his parole was over in one week. My dad wanted him to leave when his parole was up. From previous experiences, my dad had learned that ex-cons were not reliable workers after their parole was up. Also, I knew my mother was afraid of him and had become more alarmed after the episode in the middle of the night when the dead intruder's gang had chased him. She wanted him gone. I was very saddened by the news. He had become a friend who was fun to work with. I also knew we would never get another worker like him.

"Don'ts cries, Little Brudder." Leslie said jokingly.

He explained to me that it was for the best, because now he could leave town without it looking too suspicious. Besides, he would not have to report to a parole officer anymore. Plus, the gang that hung out in the Paris Inn were already suspicious and would be after him.

"Where will you go?"

"Petersburg! Dere's a woman dere dat wants to get down wit me." Leslie said with a big smile.

Leslie and I got the rye in behind the corn that next week. The dairy herd would have extra fall and spring pasture from the rye. We would plow the rye up late next spring and plant another crop of silage corn and the process would start over again. It would be springtime in the Rappahannock River Valley and the herring would be running.

I knew I would be going to college the next fall and someone else would be planting the rye behind the silage corn.

I hoped that one day I would see Leslie again. Our shared secret was forever etched in my memory.

ABOUT THE AUTHOR

Emmett Snead grew up on Braehead Farm in Fredericksburg, Va. He practices the sustainable farming methods he learned from his father and grandfather at Snead's Farm in Caroline County, Va.
For more information, visit sneadsfarm.com.

Made in the USA
Columbia, SC
28 February 2018